Also by the Author

Augustine Came to Kent

by
Barbara Willard

illustrated by
Mary Beth Owens

BETHLEHEM BOOKS · IGNATIUS PRESS
BATHGATE, N.D.   SAN FRANCISCO

ISBN: 978-1-883937-21-8
Library of Congress catalog number: 96-85301

Bethlehem Books · Ignatius Press
10194 Garfield Street South
Bathgate, ND 58216
www.bethlehembooks.com

Printed in the United States on acid free paper

Manufactured by Thomson-Shore, Dexter, MI (USA); RMA82JM86, August, 2015

Table Of Contents

AUGUSTINE'S JOURNEY TO KENT

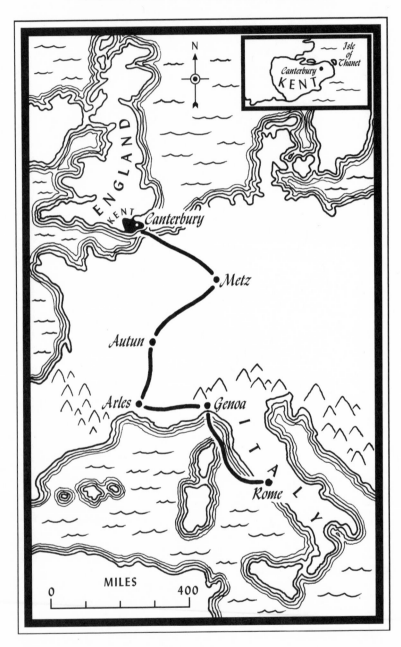

Introduction

AS A CHILD I loved the series of books entitled *He
Went with Marco Polo, He Went with Christopher
Columbus,* etc. Most children enjoy the formula of a historical novel seen through the eyes of a girl or boy their
own age. In imagination, they become part of the story.
If the story is not only historical—in this instance, set
in Rome and England at the end of the sixth and beginning of the seventh centuries—but also supernatural—
how God intervenes in history through the saints—it be-
comes a first-rate tool of instruction at many levels.

Barbara Willard has beautifully combined history and
the Christian faith in this book. With a true story-teller's
instinct, she has interwoven historical facts (you can check
them in Butler's *Lives of the Saints* for the Feast of St.
Augustine of Canterbury, May 27th) with an absorbing
fictitious tale in such a way that eager readers will take
delight in, and learn from, the great adventure of St. Augustine's mission to the land of the Angles (later England). She begins with the well-known story of the future
Pope St. Gregory the Great, passing through the Roman
market-place in A.D. 585 and inquiring about some handsome fair-haired slaves who were being sold there. On
being told they were "Angles," he replied with his fa-
mous pun: "Not Angles but angels," and resolved one

day to send a Christian mission to the pagan country of these captives who had so arrested his attention. In A.D. 597 his envoy, the future St. Augustine of Canterbury, landed in Kent with a few fellow-monks, and some interpreters. This is where the story essentially begins, told from the viewpoint of Wolf, son of Wolfstan, who Miss Willard images to have been one of the slaves seen by Gregory.

Such is the skill of the narrative—not too simplistic, nor too complicated—that it is also an excellent book to read aloud. The advantage of this is that parents can stop to expand a point—whether historical or religious—where appropriate. There are many such points where one might pause to explain or where a young reader might ask a question: why did the pagan world tolerate slavery; the "Providential" aspect of Pope Gregory's stroll in the Roman market-place; why spiritual warfare against evil does not mean actual violence or armaments; what does it mean to have a missionary vocation—all these questions arise to stretch both faith and imagination.

Miss Willard conveys a wealth of wisdom in simple dramatic pictures: Wolf, the Christian boy, part Romanized, part native, "realized a strange thing—it was simply that the stranger, Augustine, standing upright there with the cross borne at his shoulder, supported by a few unarmed men, was none the less stronger than Ethelbert, King of Kent, on whose hospitality and understanding he depended. . . ." Queen Bertha bows to her husband, but kneels to Augustine, thus showing the hierarchy of the sacred over the secular; the Christian death of Cyneog, a recently baptized Angle, so impresses his fellow Saxons with its steadfast dignity and faith, that many of them seek conversion, too.

Miss Willard deals sensitively with the romantic element in the story—the developing friendship, and later love, between Wolf and Fritha, a native girl whose uncle, Hardra, provides the "dark" side of the story, in his violent resistance to the truth. Yet again, a pattern of divine providence is shown in the Angles' response to religious vocations. Monastic life itself is shown as the immensely civilizing force it was, in the period after the collapse of the Roman Empire known as the Dark Ages: "Increasingly there was church property to be administered—farms and villages, granaries and herds, dovecots and stewponds, and the sea fishery which provided winter fare for the monks and the poor they fed in great numbers. . . ." All around Wolf lies the evidence of the Roman past—ruined villas, overgrown roads, hidden mosaic floors—but contrasted with this is the Christian future of Angle-land, with the stupendous message brought by the handful of monks: "You shall know the truth and the truth shall set you free."

FRANCIS PHILLIPS
England, 1996

AUGUSTINE CAME TO KENT

I

Men in the Market Place

"WE HAD STOOD in the market place for many hours with all the rest," Wolfstan began. He paused and frowned. "But you have heard this often. Is this the story I should tell you again?"

"Yes, it is the best!" cried Ana.

The story Wolfstan had to tell his young son and daughter was so wild and strange that it seemed to come from another world. It was indeed a true tale, and certainly it had been told many times. But as she urged her father on, Ana's eyes were already round with anticipation. Her older brother, Wolf, was sitting by the doorway in the sunshine. It was just a little after noon on a day in spring and Rome seemed to doze. But not Wolf. He was sitting cross-legged, and gripping his ankles tightly, because this tale from the past that so nearly concerned him filled him with excitement however often he heard it told.

It was, after all, the story of how a boy with a Saxon name came to be living with his family in a decent home on a Roman hillside—under the direct and benevolent patronage of Pope Gregory himself.

Wolf looked across at his father and smiled. "The sun was shining so fiercely that you were faint," he prompted.

"Faint indeed, Wolf." The interruption made Wolfstan frown. He always told the tale in simple words, for he was a plain man who had had no schooling. "Where was I?"

"You were fainting in the Roman market place, Father. In the year of Our Lord five hundred and eighty-five."

"Or thereabouts. I have forgotten . . . Eobald was in greater distress even than I. We saw two men watching us. . . ."

"They were wearing strange clothes," Ana prompted him.

"Strange clothes unlike any we had seen before, Ana. Simple and clean. As pilgrims might wear."

"And they came up to you and Eobald," cried Ana, swept away by excitement, as she always was at this point of the story, "and there was sorrow in their faces because you were a poor slave, and Eobald was a poor slave, and you would be sold to cruel masters."

"Do be quiet!" Wolf said, turning on his sister. "You spoil it all. I want to know what happened next."

"You *know* what happened next!"

"If you are going to quarrel I shall not tell the tale at all."

"Father, please. . . ."

Wolfstan looked sternly at his son and daughter. Ana was still not much more than a baby, plump and pretty as her mother had been. But Wolf was hardening already out of childhood into strong boy-hood. He had lately grown lean and tough. There was a steadiness in his eyes that showed he had be-gun to think for himself. Wolfstan thanked God for him. He remembered how nearly they had lost one another and he shuddered. Telling this old story al-ways disturbed him. But it was right that it should not be forgotten, that his children should know how much they owed to the two strangers who had walked that day at noon through the Roman slave market.

For an hour and more before they came, Wolfstan had been supporting Eobald, and for longer than that the younger man had not spoken. They had both been taken by the raiders on the same day, though from different parts of the country.

In the southern parts of the country the people had been little molested in this way, though they knew from travelers' tales that such things were common on the east and northeast coasts. Sometimes it was only the men who were taken to be sold in the slave markets of the world, but that day they took the young women and many children, too. Wolfstan had been working in the fields when the raiders—fierce marauding bands from across the seas—swooped on the village. They rounded up every soul in sight except the old people and drove them to the coast twenty miles to the south. As he was dragged off, only half conscious, Wolfstan had been aware of his young wife, Ea, screaming to him. The last thing he remembered was turning his head toward her in a final struggle with his captors and seeing her, with their young son at her side, running frantically toward him.

Later, there was the horror of the voyage. Only the men were aboard the vessel that took Wolfstan and a hundred more through plunging seas down the long coastline to Tuscany. Little more than half survived the journey. In his despair Wolfstan would have welcomed death and he was ready to contrive his own destruction. But he had helped Eobald from the start and could not abandon him. And so it had been all along, Wolfstan the tough young farmer, who had worked in the fields since he was a child, urging on Eobald, a chieftain's son, who had lived well and therefore found the ordeal twice as hard.

Caring for the lad had been a kind of distraction. But once they were penned in the Roman market place along with a great collection of strangers taken from half a dozen lands, Wolfstan had looked about him in the blazing midday and despair made him beat on his chest with his bound fists. Then he felt Eobald sagging against him, and turned his attention from his own sorrows to the immediate need of his companion. He propped the boy against his shoulder as well as he could. The sun had blistered Eobald's skin, reminding Wolfstan of his own young son's fairness that he could never hope to see again.

It was as he looked away from Eobald, hardly able to endure his own misery, that Wolfstan had seen the two strangers.

Both men were plainly dressed. Since he knew nothing of the country's customs, Wolfstan had no idea who or what they might be. Merchants or scholars, men of influence—he could not tell. All he knew was that here were two who might be prospective buyers. That told him that the midday pause for food and rest was over and the business of inspection would begin again. Buyers would move among the slaves, attended by the overseers. The merchandise would be turned about and prodded, teeth would be inspected, muscles pinched. . . . Wolfstan looked at the newcomers, and he was scowling and black with hatred.

Then, to his bewilderment, he saw the compassion in their faces. One seemed a man of importance, the other his attendant. The first asked a question, the other deferentially replied. Wolfstan heard their words but he could not understand them. Except one. It was *Angli.* That meant they were speaking of his own country, Anglia or England. His heart hammered because he realized that he and Eobald had been singled out by these strangers.

The first man summoned an overseer and spoke to him. All three moved forward, the overseer thrusting aside any in his way, sending them staggering against one another, since their hands were bound.

At last the overseer had his hand on Eobald's shoulder, jerking him upright so roughly that his head lolled.

The leader of the two men spoke one sharp word. The overseer scowled. The stranger's hand was laid on Wolfstan's arm—not in command or appraisal, but in reassurance. . . .

"And then?" cried Ana, rocking backward and forward, unable to keep quiet a moment longer.

"Then, Ana, your father knew the meaning of comfort."

"And you were taken away from the market," she cried.

"And led to a house in a cool and shady place," said Wolf.

"And you were given water and clean clothes."

"And food."

"And even poor Eobald felt better."

"And then?" said Wolf.

"And then that evening the tall stranger came where I had been left to rest, and he spoke three words in my own tongue."

"What did he say, Father?"

"He said, 'You are free.' "

That had all been a long time ago. The name of the tall stranger who had saved Wolfstan and Eobald was Gregory. The son of a Roman patrician who had hoped to see him high in the government of the country, Gregory had abandoned all wealth and comfort to become a monk of the Order of St. Benedict. Now, nearly ten years after that day in the market place, he was Pope Gregory the First. Already he was spoken of as a saint. And as a saint of goodness and mercy Wolfstan regarded him. Had he not sent messengers searching and inquiring for Ea and the boy? It was a miracle in itself that they had been found. As humble as he was great, Gregory had made the family his especial care, instructing them personally in the Christian faith, giving Wolfstan work and a house to live in and sending Wolf to the school in the monastery he had founded.

On the day Gregory, against his own wishes, was elected Pope, he sent for Wolfstan.

"I have been raised up," he said. "So shall you be."

Wolfstan was put in charge of all the monastic farms, administering them as head bailiff. He went about his work steadfastly, as always. One day, he believed, he would be given the chance to repay Pope Gregory. He knew that he and Eobald had been rescued, not only because of Gregory's bitter distaste for slavery, but also because at the sight of them he had been filled with a deep ambition.

"I was told you were Angles," he had said to Wolfstan many years ago, "but to me your fair skin and hair made you seem more like angels. I desired to bring these angels nearer heaven, and with them all their countrymen. In God's good time we shall send a mission to England to preach the gospel."

Unlike Wolfstan, who was a family man, Eobald had become a monk soon after baptism. He had been put in charge of a number of pupils and ordered to instruct them in his own language. Among them was Wolfstan's young son. The boy's name was Wolfbert. But in tribute to Rome, which had saved and supported his family, he was always called simply Wolf. Thus he and his parents saluted the city's founders, Romulus and Remus, the foster sons of the she-wolf who had saved them from death. . . .

On the day that Wolfstan was telling his young son and daughter for the hundredth time how he had been saved by Gregory, Ea his wife was sick. It was for this reason that the tale had been told yet again—to distract them and occupy them all as they sat waiting for her to wake after a soothing draught sent to her by Brother Lucian, the infirmarian at the monastery.

"When she wakes—will she be better?" Ana asked.

"We must pray so."

Wolf had so far taken the illness lightly. His mother had never been robust and often lay down with her hands held across her brow, though she never complained. His father's tone caused the boy to look up sharply and inquiringly.

"She is not very ill, is she, Father?"

"She is not well," Wolfstan replied shortly. "She suffered too much—too much."

Wolf knew he was thinking of that dreadful day

when they had been separated and carried off. In his own mind there was a muddled picture, like a half-remembered dream, of confusion and crying and darkness. But it was difficult to know what he remembered and what he had been told. He had a recollection of different surroundings, and perhaps if he saw them again he might recognize them. But for him, home had always been here. He was only a little different from his young Roman companions—fairer, certainly, and taller—and slower spoken with a faintly awkward way of mouthing his words, because his tongue had been made for a different language.

A coldness touched Wolf as he looked at his father's face. He knew suddenly that his mother might die. Once people fell sick there was often no way of curing them. Among Wolf's friends were many motherless boys but he had never thought until now that he could become one of them.

"Let's go to the river, Ana," he said. "When we come home, perhaps she will be awake."

He felt his sister's hand tremble as she slipped it into his. Without speaking again to their father, the two of them went out of the house. The hot sun of early afternoon was on their heads as they went down the hill together. Ana held Wolf's hand tightly, running to keep up with his longer stride. She was making a little sobbing noise, but there were no tears on her cheeks.

Halfway down the hill there was a fountain set in a small paved court. A boy was there, playing with colored balls that he tossed into the air three at a time, catching them in ones and twos, counting as he did so in a chanting way.

"Tullus!" cried Ana, forgetting her fears at the sight of Wolf's greatest friend. She ran forward at once. The boy was distracted and dropped the colored balls.

"Look what you have done!"

Wolf and Tullus and Ana scrambled to catch the balls before they went rolling off down the slope. Tullus was frowning and furious, but he was furious with Wolf, not Ana. He could never be cross with Ana, whatever she did. He thanked her when she handed him the blue and the gold, but he scowled at Wolf and cried angrily:

"Why not look where you're going next time! I was practicing for the fair. You've put me off now."

At the great city fair next month there would be many contests, and juggling would be one of them. Tullus had a fine eye and a steady hand for such things. Last year he had been second of all the contestants in Rome, man or boy.

"Do it again, Tullus," Ana urged him, smiling up at him so lovingly and flatteringly that he blushed.

Wolf and Ana did not get to the river after all, for they stayed with Tullus, encouraging and admiring and chasing after the balls whenever they dropped, which was fairly often, for he had lost his eye for the time being. At last he was so enraged with his failure that he gave up.

"Come home with me and see my mother. You know Ana is her favorite."

"Then I had better take myself off," groused Wolf.

Tullus chuckled, recovering his good humor. He whacked his friend amiably across the shoulders and gave him a shove up the hill. They all climbed the steep track to his home, which was set slantwise in the hillside. Geese and hens pecked and waddled on the earth terrace beside the well, and one of Tullus' several brothers was driving the donkey with a load of wood to stack in the lean-to behind the house.

Tullus' mother, Ursula, stood at the door holding her headcloth against the sun to shield her eyes. But she dropped it and held out her arms when she saw Ana. And Ana rushed to her and was swept up in a huge embrace.

"Ah, the little dear, the little bird!" cried Ursula, who had no daughter but only six great strapping sons. "Oh, she smells so warm—like a little honey cake! I could eat the little creature!"

And she nibbled at Ana's ears, first one then the other in such rapid turns that the child laughed.

Watching them together, Wolf thought of his own mother. If she should die—perhaps Ursula would be another mother to Ana? When he had thought of this, Wolf felt, not happier certainly, but less like a very old man carrying a heavy burden up a steep hill.

Presently it was time to go. Now the heat of the spring sunshine had gone and the evening was cool and calm. They walked slowly back to their own home. The goats tethered in the shade of the yard wall were bleating strongly.

"Time they were milked," said Wolf. "We should

have come home sooner." For it was his job to look after the goats.

Their father came from the house as they hurried toward it.

"Where have you been? Listen to the goats."

But he was smiling.

"Is she awake?" Wolf asked.

Wolfstan nodded contentedly. "And the fever has gone. Go in to her. I will start the milking."

Wolf laughed and ran indoors after Ana. Ea was still lying on her bed, but they saw at once that she was refreshed and comfortable.

"I woke an hour ago and called for you."

"We were with Tullus and his mother," Ana said.

Ea smiled at Wolf over Ana's fair head.

"Take care, Wolf, or you will lose your sister to Tullus."

"He is clever," Ana said, "the cleverest boy in all Rome. Wolf cannot juggle like Tullus."

"I can throw a javelin straighter. And farther."

"But the colored balls are much prettier than a javelin."

"Very well, Ana. I must learn to juggle, I suppose."

"But you will never, never be so good as Tullus."

"Listen," said Ea. "Your father is talking to some-one. Go quickly and see if there is anything he needs."

Wolf was already at the door and looking down the path.

"It is one of the brothers. Brother Septimus, I think. He has brought a jar of honey. That will be for you, Mother."

"Go quickly and greet him, Wolf."

Wolf ran out of the house, but as he reached the roadway Brother Septimus turned away and set off down the hill.

Wolfstan raised his hand in farewell and then came toward the house. He held the honey jar brought by Brother Septimus. He looked thoughtful, so thoughtful that he was more than halfway to frowning. Some business about the farms, Wolf supposed, that his father must attend to.

"Bring me a pitcher of water before you do the milking," Wolfstan called to his son. "I must go out. Pope Gregory has bidden me. I must go at once."

"What is the matter, then?"

"How can I say? And how should it concern you?" Wolfstan replied sharply.

"Father, I only meant—"

"Stop talking and bring me the water. Do you expect me to go unwashed to speak with the Holy Father?"

Five minutes later he left the house and strode off.

Wolf was milking by then. He frowned after his father and without thinking what he was doing pulled so sharply at the goat's full udder that she kicked. He nearly overturned himself and the pail. He soothed the creature quickly. She blinked her long lashes at him warily. Wolf tried to concentrate on the job, but his mind was wandering. It was a curious time of day for his father to be summoned. Wolf felt uneasy because he knew Wolfstan had been uneasy too.

II

News of a Journey

EOBALD was at the door when Wolfstan reached the monastery, where he had been told to attend Pope Gregory.

"God be with you," said Eobald—or Brother Sylvanus, as Wolfstan had long become accustomed to calling him.

"And with you, Brother."

Wolfstan's reply was a shade absent-minded. Brother Sylvanus was doubtless humble enough in his approach to God, but he had little use for those he considered beneath him. He had forgotten the dreadful days of the voyage in the slave trader's galley. He had forgotten that Wolfstan had cared for him then, that he might well be said to owe his life to the older man. The one thing Brother Sylvanus could not forget was that in England he had been a chieftain's son. His breeding fitted him for learning. His profession as a monk came soon after his baptism, and his promotion followed as rapidly. He was clever, well suited to be confidant and secretary to Pope Gregory himself, as well as head of studies in his own native tongue.

Wolfstan would never have denied these things. He respected the abilities of his countryman. But try as he would he could not swallow that air of lofty disdain. In his own way Wolfstan was just as responsible to Pope Gregory as Brother Sylvanus himself. But his was a yeoman task, the task of a man who had never been taught to read or write and whose capabilities did not qualify him to learn. He worked by instinct. His skills were inherited skills—the care of beasts and the growing of grain. Wolfstan could not have attempted Brother Sylvanus' work, but he wished that Sylvanus would admit his own inability to do Wolfstan's.

"The Holy Father is waiting," Brother Sylvanus said now. "Hurry."

"I came at once. Would you have me greet him with unwashed hands?"

He spoke ironically, for he knew Sylvanus thought of him as a farmer whose hands were forever soiled and stained with his occupation. Brother Sylvanus did not reply. He went ahead of Wolfstan across the courtyard where fountains played in the still cool evening. The Monastery of St. Anthony had been Pope Gregory's family home. Stripped now of its richest ornaments, it remained a place of great beauty. Tall cypresses grew on either side of paved walks, and from the terraces you could look out over the city to the farther hills and see the mist lying upon the river's face at dusk and dawn.

Vaguely worried as he was by the unexpected summons, Wolfstan followed so briskly where he was led that Sylvanus had to hurry his dignified steps or have his fellow countryman tread upon his heels. A faint smile softened Wolfstan's rather grim expression. Then the smile turned to a shamefaced grin as he realized that he would want to tell the tale of Brother Sylvanus' discomfort to his children.

Pope Gregory was walking in one of the long avenues of cypress, with a tall thin man at his side.

"Wait here, Wolfstan."

Wolfstan stood and watched the monk walk away between the trees. Before he was halfway to the Pope, Gregory and his companion turned and began pacing back the way they had come, then stopped as Sylvanus reached them and spoke, bowing to the Pope.

At once Gregory put his hand on his companion's

arm. They both stood looking past Sylvanus to where Wolfstan waited. Gregory said something to his companion, then at once beckoned Wolfstan. He was smiling. The appearance he gave, of welcoming an old and valued friend, took away the bitter taste that had been in Wolfstan's mouth since he encountered Brother Sylvanus.

Without waiting for any further summons, Wolfstan went smiling toward Pope Gregory, remembering to drop on one knee when he reached him—instead, as he would have preferred, of clasping both his hands in grateful friendship.

"God and his servant bless you, Wolfstan," Gregory said. "Now rise up quickly and look long and hard upon this brother beside me. Do you know him?"

"Of course, Holy Father. It is the Father Prior. It is Father Augustine."

"Yes, it is Augustine. And he is to be my active self. He is to fulfill my dearest ambition while I must remain behind in Rome. He is going to take you home, Wolfstan, my friend."

When Wolfstan returned to his own house it was in darkness save for one small glimmer. With a saucer of oil burning on the ground beside him, Wolf was lying on a mat on the porch. He was watching for his father's return, but he had fallen asleep as the time wore away. He was curled as comfortably as a calf in straw, Wolfstan thought. He sighed. What had been offered him had been hard to refuse. Even now he was uncertain that he had been right to refuse it.

Looking down at Wolf he saw first a young boy who must still be cared for and cherished and second a boy who was already becoming a man and who might himself have chosen differently.

As Wolfstan stepped past his son, Wolf stirred and was instantly awake.

"Father?"

"Go back to sleep."

"But I am awake now!" Wolf looked at his father, wondering if he dared ask a question. He saw that Wolfstan was worried, concerned with something Wolf knew nothing about. An immense sympathy for his father swelled up in his heart. He felt for a moment as though they were nearer to being brothers than father and son. And it was this that made him ask, not boldly or inquisitively, but simply as if he had a right to know: "What did the Holy Father say to you?"

"Prior Augustine was with him. . . ." Wolfstan hesitated, as though uncertain how much he could tell the boy. "He is a great preacher."

"Did he preach to you this evening, then?"

"No. It was not for that I was called." Wolfstan sighed. Then he joined Wolf on the mat, and the pair of them sat side by side, their backs against the wall. "Pope Gregory has one dear wish. For many years it has been so. Now it will be fulfilled."

"Is it the mission to our country?" Wolf asked.

His father looked at him curiously in the dim light of the passageway. Wolf felt himself turning red. He looked upon himself as a Roman; here his home had been for as long as he could remember; though he was fairer than his young companions and spoke with a slightly different inflection, he was accepted as one of them—indeed, he would have been deeply wounded if any had treated him as a stranger. And yet in this moment of confidence in the dark midnight, he spoke of our country, and meant the island in which he had been born.

Wolfstan nodded. "Yes. It is the mission to England. You know as I do that Pope Gregory, when he was still a plain monk, wished to lead such a mission himself. The people would not let him go. Now at last he has chosen a leader—Prior Augustine—"

Wolf broke in. "Are we to go with him?"

"My boy, I cannot leave Rome while your mother is sick. I have told the Holy Father."

"I understand," Wolf said, ashamed of his disappointment. "He will understand too."

"But I know I should pay my debt. I speak my native tongue. This would be of great value. For this I was saved from the slave market and given my freedom. God help me, I should pay my debt."

At this moment they heard Ea stir and call out. Wolfstan rose at once to go to her. He touched his son's head as he left him.

"It is between the two of us. Say nothing."

When his father had gone and the house once more was silent, Wolf lay back on the mat with his hands behind his head and stared at the shadow cast by the lamp on the wall near him.

Perhaps this was the first time Wolf had given himself up to serious thought. Ordinarily he was occupied

with active matters. He had his own work to do about
the place, not only the goats but other tasks he did
for his mother and Esta, the old woman who had
come to cook when Ea first became too ill. Every
morning at seven, he and twenty or so boys, children
of fathers employed like his own on the domestic affairs of the monastery, went to lessons presided over
by Brother Severus. They worked until noon. Later,
Wolf and two others—but they were poor pupils—went
to speak the English tongue with Brother Sylvanus.
Wolf was always glad to be released from lessons, but
he was interested in serious games like running and
throwing, and in swimming and diving and wrestling.
He loved his life in Rome without ever pausing to
think that he loved it. He was fortunate. His father had
good employment, the family was well housed and
well fed. His father was respected for honesty and up-
rightness and great good judgment. His mother was
held in affection by the other women and never criti-
cized or derided as a stranger from a barbarous land
where men had rejected the teachings of Christ and
returned to the worship of false gods.

For the first time, lying there in the half dark, Wolf
found himself questioning all this. However much he
might owe to Rome, it was not his native country, as
it was his sister's, as it was his friend Tullus'. Somewhere in the dark forgotten places of his memory
there was another land, not always sunny, harshly
troubled by invasion and pillage and paganism. And
suddenly it seemed wrong that this land meant more
to Pope Gregory, who had never set foot in it, than

to Wolf, who had been born there and been torn from it by force.

He saw his father pass just out of range of the feeble lamplight, carrying a pitcher to fill at the well. Wolf rose and followed him outside.

It was a warm night and very still. Looking out over the terraced hillside was like looking into a mighty pool above which the stars hung hugely. Wolf could see his father's dark figure in the starlight, stooping at the well, hauling, lifting the full pitcher which splashed back some water into the darkness below.

"Father—"

"Get into the house and sleep. How will you do your lessons in the morning?"

"When will they go to England?"

"When they are ready. Soon."

"Before the summer fair?" asked Wolf.

"What has the summer fair to do with Pope Gregory, Father Augustine and England?" demanded Wolfstan, half laughing.

"Tullus may win the juggling. I would sooner be there to see him."

"What should stop you?"

"I could go to England. I could go in your place."

Starlight or no, it was too dark for Wolf to see his father's face.

"They do say a son may pay his father's debts," Wolfstan said, shouldering the pitcher.

"Then—shall I?"

"Wait until the morning, my son. We are all brave

in the dark. Come, now. You must sleep. Wait until the morning."

When morning came, Wolfstan was away from the house and about his work by the time Wolf woke. Esta was pulling loaves from the oven as the boy went yawning outside. The smell of the hot bread filled the air and sharpened his appetite. He went to the well and drew himself some water, and plunged his face into it and splashed the water over his head and neck and arms.

"Hurry," said the old woman. "You'll be late for school. Brother Severus will beat you."

Wolf did not reply. He had remembered the mission and his heart thumped. He felt bold at once.

"Give me some bread."

"You shall have it when you ask decently. What would your poor mother say if she heard you speak like that to an old woman?"

"You talk too much. You know too many words. You said I was late. Give me the bread to eat as I go."

"Here, then." She grumbled to herself as she sorted the loaves and chose what she thought fitting for him.

Then he saw his mother at the door. She moved slowly, holding on to the wall. She was pale and her hollow eyes looked almost black. Wolf thrust the hot bread inside his shirt and ran to her.

"How tall you have grown, Wolf. I saw how tall as you stood beside old Esta."

"And I am tall beside you, too, Mother. I could carry you all the way across the city on my back and not know it!"

"Well, you shall do so one day. When I feel a little stronger." She smiled at him. "Now get off with you to your lessons."

"Give me your blessing, then, Mother," he said, quickly kneeling.

Her hands on his head were as light and thin as last year's leaves.

"May God bless you, my dearest son."

A terrible fear made Wolf tremble. Not daring to look at her, he stumbled to his feet and rushed away. When he reached the gate of the monastery he discovered that he had not had one bite of bread. He knew, now, why his father could not leave Ea and go with the mission to England. He knew, also, that he was, after all, not brave enough to go himself.

It was not so long since the Lombards, the people dwelling in the great northern plain, had risen under their warlike king and battled their way down through the length of Italy until they stood at the very gates of Rome. For hundreds of miles the countryside had been ravaged by these people. The wisdom of Gregory, his counsel and brave admonishment of the savage King of the Lombards, had saved the city from destruction. Already the occasion had taken on the glory of a legend, and there were those eager to claim this as a miracle proving that a saint moved among them.

Famine and pestilence had followed the terrible destruction of the countryside. Wolfstan could speak of that, but for young Wolf there were no such memories. He had grown in the confidence and contentment of

a secure home, and the years of his childhood were
years of recovery. Now granaries were full once more
and order prevailed in the city and countryside close
by.

Further afield, however, beyond the hills that circled
and contained the Holy City, there was an incessant
small warfare. Skirmishing and pillaging made travel
dangerous and difficult.

"How will they fare as they cross the great plains,
as they journey toward the sea or the mountains?"

This was the question heard on all sides as news
of the mission to the distant island spread among the
people.

"They will never return. They will never reach
the barbarians' country, never reach the mountains,
never cross the sea."

In spite of these gloomy prophecies, the mission
was planned and ordered within a short time. For
although the men who set out would be preparing
for a battle, their weapons were not heavy to carry,
being their own wits and their faith and their steadfast courage. Nor was there any lack of laymen ready
to accompany the monks as ostlers and smiths and
the like. The adventure drew them. They would step
out into the unknown. Though it might swallow them,
yet they could not resist its enticement. Some people
considered that these men should not be included in
the mission at all, that it was for the monks alone to
take all responsibility. But the size of the community
was such that too great a number could not be withdrawn. As it was, forty men in all would make up

the mission, and of these about two-thirds were professed monks.

It was Wolfstan's job to order the stores, to select little sturdy horses accustomed to long journeying, and pack mules to carry the burdens.

"Brother Severus is to go with them," Wolf told his friend Tullus.

"Then we shall have no lessons!" cried Tullus, overjoyed at the news.

"Oh, there is a new schoolmaster. It is Brother Hugo, who comes from beyond the Elbe. My father has seen him. He is short and fat and looks merry—so he says."

If he could not go with the mission, Wolf at least had the pleasure of passing on information to his friends.

Besides Brother Severus there were others known to Wolf among the missionaries. There was, of course, the Englishman, Eobald—or Brother Sylvanus—who had been a chieftain's son. He would be guide and interpreter when they came to his native land. There was Brother Lucian, one of the infirmarians, and Brother Adrian, a cook. And others Wolf knew only by seeing them about the cloisters when he went on some message for his father.

The mission set out for Rome at dawn on a morning in late May. Wolf was up as early as his father and the pair of them went to the monastery chapel. There was not room for all of those who had come, and they knelt about the open doors, joining in as well as they could. Pope Gregory himself said the

Mass that dedicated the mission and prayed for its
success. He did so, less as the Sovereign Pontiff than
as the abbot of that monastic house which he had
founded in his own home—the place of all places in
the world toward which his spirit turned, from which
he had been drawn reluctantly to take up his great
office.

Kneeling outside in the quiet dawn, fidgeting as
the rough ground bit his knees, Wolf thought less of
his prayers than of what lay ahead for these men. He
longed to be going with them. He wished with all
his heart that he might set out with the rest, secure
in his father's company, having said farewell to a mother
strong enough to bear the parting, healthy enough
to expect with confidence their return. In his mind
he saw all England as a place of great darkness, as
though thick forest grew everywhere and hid the light
from the native peoples. He thought again, *My country, and I must go to it.* It could not be now, but he
prayed that it might be soon.

Round about him, the people rose up and drew
back on either side as the monks came in procession
from the chapel. At the gates of the monastery, as
Wolf knew, the horses and mules would be assem-
bled and his father would be there with them, check-
ing the stores and seeing that everything was in order.
The head of the procession, young Brother Antonius
carrying the cross, now stepped from the chapel into
the increasing morning. After him came six of the
senior brethren. After them, walking alone, Augustine
the leader.

He was a tall man and seemed at this moment to have gained stature over everyone else about him. His face was grave but calm. Though he had tucked his hands into his sleeves modestly, his eyes looking straight ahead were more proud than humble; there was courage in his face and a burning light that must surely inspire all who saw it.

Yet looking at him as he passed, Wolf waited in vain to feel affection well up in him—for that kind of love which a dedicated leader can often call up in his followers. Wolf felt a great respect, a great awe, but he could not imagine this man of God as his friend.

As the procession moved off, Wolf began to run alongside. Halfway to the gates, he found Tullus running with him. They shot through the gateway ahead of the procession and took up their places on a high bank opposite.

At the gateway the ranks broke as the monks consulted about the stores and the animals. Then they re-formed in a new order. Augustine mounted and moved off at a walking pace. The rest led their animals, and the pack mules and servants followed.

The crowd now began to move in a disorderly way. Where all had been silent and awestruck, now they started to cry out blessings and farewells. Some were the families of those leaving for their unknown future—parents and sisters of monks, the wives of two of the ostlers, young women who wept and wailed together at the loss of their husbands—who seemed to care very little at leaving them, and kept their eyes fixed firmly ahead, as though only the future had any claims on them.

Slowly the procession gained on the crowd as more of the monks took to their horses. There was an increasing clatter of hooves on the cobbles, then the deadened thud of hooves on dust. The voices of the crowd became louder; their praises became a lament. Their hurrying ceased and they fell back at last, first to a jog trot, then to a walk, then to a silent stillness. The noise of the horses was taken into the quiet of early morning as the sun increased, rising and flooding the city and the city's hills with radiance. Gradually the crowd broke up. In ones and twos those who were left behind moved off toward their homes. Soon no one was left but a very old woman kneeling in the roadway, staring after what was vanished, as motionless as if she had died there on her knees. Then at last she, too, rose slowly and stiffly to her feet, and straightened her back painfully, and shuffled away.

"If I had gone," said Wolf to Tullus, as they scrambled down from their high perch, "would you have come too?"

Tullus shook his head very firmly. "I am not a monk and England is not my country, praise be. And even for friendship's sake—well, I would sooner stay and win the juggling at the fair!"

Wolf gave him a shove that sent him sprawling down the bank with a shout of surprise.

"So much for friendship!" cried Wolf, roaring with laughter.

Behind them there was a clash and a clang as the

porter, Brother Andreas, closed the great gates and bolted them, then rattled his huge key into the lock and turned it to make all secure. The mission had departed and the monastery must return to its daily routine. Once more, the world was shut out.

Wolf and Tullus went slowly homeward. Both experienced a feeling of flatness. The rest of the day remained, and for them it would be a day like any other day, except that lessons would be presided over by the new teacher, Brother Hugo.

III

The Second Chance

"**P**AY ATTENTION!" said Brother Hugo, walking between the rows of scholars as he talked. "Wolf, you are dreaming. Pay attention."

Brother Hugo had turned out badly after all. His apparent merriment was nothing better than a kind of sarcasm. His fatness lent strength to blows he was free in dealing.

"Attention," he repeated. "God expects us to accept our opportunities. Work, then. Attend to what I say. The world is waiting for wise and learned men strong in their faith. See to it that you are ready, for the call may come to you."

His hand had fallen on Wolf's shoulder. Impatiently, for he was much preoccupied, Wolf shrugged it off.

"So you reject my words?" Brother Hugo's sharp, sudden temper rose instantly. "Have a care, my son."

Wolf in fact had barely heard what his master was saying. He was thinking about his mother. On that morning when she had seen him for the first time as a tall lad growing into manhood, Wolf in his turn had seen her as a woman not only sick but dying. And since that day she had declined still more. He knew it. His misery filled him until he seemed to feel it even in the pores of his skin. It had become almost impossible for him to work at school. Brother Hugo, having to take charge of him at that moment, could hardly be blamed for thinking him stupid and lazy.

"Attention, I say! Attention! Pay attention to me, Wolf!"

And each time he said *attention* Brother Hugo cuffed Wolf smartly about the ears.

Wolf's head sang with the blows. His eyes were hot with rage and pride. He wished he might strike back. Beside him he could feel Tullus bursting with sympathetic rage. Wolf remembered how he had offered to go to England in his father's place, how he had imagined himself strong enough. What a fool he felt, thinking of the offer now. He was a schoolboy still, at the mercy of his masters, and he must remain so for a long while to come.

Brother Hugo turned about sharply, as though he might strike Wolf again unless he controlled himself.

"Attend to your tasks," he ordered the class. "Tullus, eyes on your book. Do not lift your heads, any one of you, until I give permission."

It was half an hour short of noon when the porter, Brother Andreas, came to speak to Brother Hugo. He talked to him quietly and hurriedly. As he did so, he glanced toward the scholars, who dared not lift their eyes to see what the interruption might mean. But keeping their heads down, they managed still to squint up under their lashes and to discuss the porter's errand in whispers out of the sides of their mouths.

"Last time, it was a holiday."

"The time before it was a beating for Josephus for stealing fruit."

"He doesn't look at all stern."

"He looks fairly sad. Perhaps—"

At that Wolf suddenly raised his head. As he did so, he saw both the brothers looking toward him.

Automatically, as though they had called him, Wolf rose and stepped forward.

"Wolf—"

"Is it my mother?"

"Yes, my child." Now Brother Hugo's voice was gentle enough. "Go home at once. Go quickly."

Wolf ran. Brother Hugo was still saying something, but he could not wait to hear. He ran across the courtyard where the sun struck harshly on the back of his neck. Down the long avenue to the gateway, where he had to wait after all for Brother Andreas to catch up with him and unlock the gate.

"Hurry!" Wolf cried. "Hurry!"

And although he was only one of the young scholars, the porter indeed made haste for him. Wolf slipped through the gate before it was properly open and went pelting in the direction of home. As he came within sight of the place he saw a knot of people gathered outside. He stopped short. He was filled with terror at what he might find and he almost turned and ran away. Surely he could hide somewhere until it was all over?

But Ursula, Tullus' mother, was among the crowd and saw him. She ran toward him, holding out both hands, and he could not escape then.

"Is she dead?" His voice was so harsh and ringing that everyone turned. "Hush," someone said.

"Yes, my darling, my boy. Your mother is dead. Peacefully, peacefully, my child. If ever God was with a dying woman, He was with Ea. Go in now to your father."

Wolf shrank away. "Where is Ana?"

"I have taken her home. My son's wife is caring

for her. Leave her with me for a while. She is too young for this sorrow. Come now, Wolf. Your father needs you."

She put her arm round him and urged him forward. His feet dragged and made a little shuffle of dust about him. The crowd of neighbors and friends fell back to let him pass. On the threshold, Ursula pressed Wolf's hands hard and gave him a gentle push inside, remaining herself with the rest.

Wolf stood inside the doorway. The house seemed very dark. He waited to hear some sound, but there was nothing. He remembered that when his schoolfellow Marcius' mother died, the house had been filled with wailing. Marcius had told him about it, and how his father had sobbed and thrown himself on the ground, refusing to eat. Yet here was silence.

Wolf forced himself to go forward. He went into the little chamber where his mother had so often lain in sickness, not complaining, but as it were shut away from them all. Wolfstan was standing, looking down at the bed, and there Ea lay as quietly and sweetly as if she slept. Esta was crouched close by, rocking herself to and fro, her veil drawn over her face, but silent in deference to the silence Wolfstan had imposed upon himself.

"Father," Wolf said.

Wolfstan did not turn, but he held out his hand. Wolf took it in both his and they clasped one another in this way, Wolf turning his head over his shoulder rather than see Ea lying dead. Then Wolfstan slipped his arm across the boy's shoulders and drew him closer.

"She is smiling, Wolf. She was asleep and dreaming, and smiling at her dream, when she died. Come now, kneel with me and thank Almighty God."

"For taking her?" Wolf cried, his voice giving a dreadful crack of rage and misery.

"For letting us keep her so long," his father corrected him. "Come."

Wolf knelt down. He heard his father's strong voice praying, not in the Roman tongue but in his own, using short blunt words. The boy's grief suddenly rose up like a wave of sickness. He clutched at his father and toppled against him. He seemed to feel himself sliding down into a deep lake full of black and bitter water. . . .

It was many hours before Wolf opened his eyes. Evening had come. He was lying on his bed, and the sunlight, gold and declining, was painting the opposite wall. Old Esta was beside him. She was dipping a cloth in cold water and wringing it and then laying it across his forehead.

"Esta—"

"Be strong," she said.

He thought it strange that she should say this—an old bad-tempered bundle of a servant-woman who frequently screamed at him for his teasing and thoughtless ways. He was ashamed.

"I am strong."

"Like your father. He is a strong strange man. His

grief will not come from him. It sits in his head and his heart like a toad. They say it is because he came from the North. He is still a stranger among us and we cannot know his ways."

"Yes," said Wolf, "he is from England. From England. That is my country. I shall go there one day."

As he spoke, Wolf remembered all his father had ever told him of that country. He had heard it so often that he almost believed the memories were his own. Did he indeed remember something? Did he remember the low hills, the forest glades, the house built of stone and the smoke from the hearth rising up through the hole in the roof? It was certain he had never seen the beautiful crumbling cities that the Romans built when they had occupied the land they left to rot. When they withdrew to their own country, Britain was left defenseless. Brother Sylvanus had often spoken of this. Then had come the enemy swooping down from harsh countries across the northern seas, battering mercilessly at a people left to look after itself after years of subjection. In the darkness that followed, even the light of Christianity had gone out in all but a few strongholds, and men had set up idols once more to worship with pagan ferocity. . . .

These things filled Wolf's mind to overflowing. He rolled over on his face and hid his eyes, and Esta thought he was struggling with his grief. But he dared not even consider what had happened to him yet. Instead he thought of England, of Pope Gregory's long desire to bring a whole people back to God. He thought of Father Augustine and the rest who, even now, were on their way to preach to that people. If he had had a fine swift horse in a well-kept stable, Wolf told himself, he would have leaped into the saddle and ridden fast for mile upon mile until he came up with the missionaries.

But that was a boy's dream and he knew it. It was too late to think of such things now.

In the home now were only Wolfstan and Wolf, with Esta to cook and clean. Ana had remained with Ursula.

"I would keep her for always, as well you know," she told Wolfstan. "My sons love her as much as I do—not only Tullus, but even the eldest of all who has children of his own. Let her stay, Wolfstan, for as long as you will."

In the weeks following his mother's death, Wolf grew up. He felt taller, stronger, harder. He withdrew from his friends and seemed to live a life of his own. They were bewildered by this. They understood and respected his grief, but they were young, as he was, and they expected him to recover quickly. And they tried to lure him into their games, only to meet with a harsh refusal. In this way gradually he lost their sympathy. They felt that his grief had made him too proud.

One midday Wolfstan came into the house and found Wolf there.

"No lessons today?"

"I had to speak to you, Father. There was something I heard. . . . I must ask you about it."

Wolfstan half frowned, half smiled.

"Do we hear with the same ears?"

"Then you have heard? About Father Augustine? They are saying he is here in Rome—that the mission has failed. Then he has abandoned our country!"

"No. They have had misfortunes by the way. Their servants have deserted them—their stores have been stolen. Father Augustine has lodged the brethren in France, at Arles, under the protection of the Bishop, and returned for instructions. He does not know how far he should risk the monks."

"What will the Holy Father say to that? What will Father Augustine do now?"

"He is to return, Wolf. He and Pope Gregory have talked together. They have prayed together. Now Father Augustine is strengthened and sure. Tomorrow at dawn, he sets out once more. There will be no turning back now."

Wolf hesitated, trying to read his father's face.

"Father, you know so much. . . ."

"I, too, have been with Pope Gregory." Wolfstan looked at his son, and this time he was indeed smiling, though with that reserve that had remained with him ever since Ea's death. "Wolf, my son, I have been given a second chance. Few men are so lucky. There is nothing to hold me now. Your mother is gone. Ana is happy with Ursula. I have made up my mind. I have said I will go with Father Augustine."

"But—what about me?"

"What about you?" cried Wolfstan. "You told me you would go. Have you changed your mind?"

IV

A Distant Land

WOLFSTAN had been given the task of finding lay servants to join the mission in place of those who had defaulted.

"They look a sorry bunch, Father Augustine. But they swear they will be loyal."

51

"God will inspire them when the time comes."

"If you ask me," replied Wolfstan, in the blunt way he had been born with, "it was the Devil himself who inspired the last lot. Or why else did they desert and leave you and the brothers without stores or protection?"

"The fault lay with me—God knows it. But thanks to the Holy Father I am strengthened and renewed.... But what about the boy? He is young for so arduous a journey. We are forging a chain, Wolfstan, and we must have no weak links. Is your son hardy? Does he understand what he is about to undertake?"

"He understands, Father. I will take care of him. He speaks the tongue, his native tongue. He can be useful."

"Well, God will see to it, if He wills. It is Pope Gregory's wish that the boy comes with us. There is no more to be said."

When Augustine first set out on his mission he had been proudly sure of his purpose. The defection of his servants, the fears of his brethren had shaken him to the point of doubting his own powers. No one would ever know what torments of conscience he had endured before he returned to Rome for further instruction. He had done so for the sake of his brethren; that he had had to do so at all was proof of some weakness in his leadership.

But now, after the long counsels and gentle admonitions of Pope Gregory, Augustine was more than merely confirmed in his mission. Now he had twice his old strength, twice his physical powers. Even his stride had lengthened, and his voice was loud with a challenge that any man must find hard to resist. His faith was like a mighty wave of the sea, engulfing all before it. . . .

There were times on that journey from Rome to Genoa on the northwest coast when Wolf clutched at his father's hand like a terrified child. Then the great plain of Lombardy, scorched and battered by perpetual warfare and raiding, seemed too cruel ever to let them pass. There were moments when the high places of the countryside seemed to echo with the wicked cries of demons, but others when the soft and star-filled night held only the voice of God.

It was a long way, fair or foul, from the life Wolf had known. He missed Ana most bitterly. Had they done right to leave her? She was happy with Ursula, who loved her so dearly. But now she would become all Roman and her native blood would be forgotten. Tullus would be her brother now. As he thought of this, Wolf could have cried with jealousy of both Tullus and Ana.

Suddenly his own true land was so distant that he knew he might never return to see his sister again. Why had he come? What ties could bind him to a country he could not even truly remember? In his heart he knew very well that he was as weak as the worst of those men who had joined as servants of the mission for their own purposes and deserted when the way became too hard. Because he had not wanted to see his father go without him, Wolf realized miserably, he had condemned Ana to do without both of them.

These were days when Wolf was as silent and withdrawn as Father Augustine himself.

But in spite of doubts, and of the sheer physical struggle of the journey, they reached the coast and crossed the sea to France, then journeyed on to that fine city of Arles where the brothers were lodged in a monastery, waiting in fear and doubt and self-accusation for the return of their leader. The brothers had had almost too much time for meditation. Their fears now were the bitter fears of remorse. Their cowardice had sent Augustine back over the dangerous way home to Rome. If he had not survived, then his death must lie heavily on their souls.

So when the first word of his return reached them, they surged out of the city to meet Augustine and carry him back with them to the cloister, there to beg his forgiveness and hear him accept their penitence.

But when they came up with the small cavalcade, they learned that Augustine had turned aside and gone to the Bishop's palace, there to deliver letters from His Holiness, Pope Gregory.

"He'll come to you all in good time," Wolfstan told them. "Wait for him in the cloister, he says. He has word for you, too, from the Holy Father."

The priory in which they were lodged was, like their own, a house of the Benedictine rule. That evening was still and thundery and as the monks waited for their leader they were restless and uneasy.

"God knows we have sinned sorely in our cowardice. Who are we to expect easy pardon?"

"But the hand of God seemed almost to be against us. We were sorely tried."

"We were tempted, Brother, and we fell."

In the center courtyard Wolfstan and the other servants were discussing supplies with the butler and porters of the priory. Helped by a young lay brother of the house, Wolf was tying up sacks, as grain and meal were inspected and counted. These were stores offered freely by the townsfolk for the support of the mission and their inspection now was the first indication that the journey would continue.

As he listened to the murmuring conversation of the waiting monks, Wolf realized with surprise that these men, grown and dedicated as they were, had been as filled with fear of the journey as he, who must seem a child to them. Little as he himself knew of the land toward which they traveled, he spoke the tongue at least. But these brothers had no word of it to help them. It was a great and alarming project they had undertaken, and if they had flagged and failed a little, who would blame them? Surely God would not.

There was a sudden stirring at the cloister entry. Above the quickly bowed heads of the monks, Wolf saw Augustine stride in. They fell back to let him through, and he moved to one of the little stone bays in the cloister wall which were places for rest and study. He stood there, waiting. Gradually everyone moved toward him, uneasily, humbly, anxiously, and then came to rest, looking toward him in hope and in fear. An intense stillness held the cloister, a silence that was only increased by a whirr of wings as six or seven doves flew over to their loft above the stable.

Then Augustine spoke. His voice was harsh and commanding and it penetrated to the farther cracks and corners of the cloister and into the minds and hearts of those who listened.

"I returned to His Holiness and told him of our fears. Our Holy Father the Pope admonished me, and to you, his children, he wrote thus—"

Augustine paused to unroll the parchment, and a breath of anticipation ran among the gathering. Then he began to read:

"Gregory, the servant of the servants of God, to the servants of Our Lord." Again there was a stirring, more like a groan than a whisper, then utter silence. "Forasmuch as it had been better not to begin a good work than to think of desisting from that which has been begun, it behoves you, my beloved sons, to fulfill the good work which, by the help of Our Lord, you have undertaken. Let not, therefore, the tongues of evil-speaking men deter you. . . . With all possible earnestness and zeal perform that which, by God's direction, you have undertaken. . . ." Then the letter spoke of Augustine "your chief, whom we also constitute your Abbot," and of how he must be obeyed in all things. At which many of the monks covered their faces and beat their breasts in penitence. "Almighty God protect you," wrote Pope Gregory, "and grant that I may, in the heavenly country, see the fruits of your labor. . . . God keep you in safety, my most beloved sons."

The letter was ended but the silence was unbroken. Augustine seemed to hold the hearts and the minds of all there as firmly as if they had been poured into his hands like coin to spend as he would. As they looked toward him they saw him then as more than a leader; they saw him as a promised saint. Through him, they too were ennobled.

Augustine spoke and the silence sighed itself away.

"Tomorrow, brethren, we continue our journey."

They had many miles and hundreds of miles to travel over rough country before they came to the coast. From Arles, in Provence, to Autun, then eastward to Metz to greet the Bishop from Pope Gregory—and so at last to the channel coast.

With Wolfstan in charge of practical traveling matters, there was no further trouble with servants or stores on the long journey north. Wolf for the best part of the time helped Brother Adrian, the cook.

"A kitchen boy is something I have long needed, and never hoped to see again. They tell me I have ideas too grand for a monastic kitchen." Brother Adrian was a small dark man, thin with enormous eyes—not perhaps Wolf's idea of how a cook should look. "The truth is, I worked in a certain rich household before I was professed. My master was Proconsul. There were fifteen cooks. Fifteen. To remember those banquets is a sin in itself."

"But this bread is good enough for now, Brother. And the meat smells wonderfully succulent."

Brother Adrian frowned and looked gloomy. "Then I had better burn it a shade or there'll be gluttony among us."

At that time they had been making camp in the open near a great forest and all that was needed was a meal made for the moment and no crumbs over, save what the birds could eat. It was not always so. Sometimes they came to other monasteries and were welcomed there. Sometimes they were obliged to make do with what shelter they could find; it might be that nothing better than a cave protected them from the weather. Winter caught up with them as they traveled, and the thought of the sea crossing ahead filled them with alarm. When they reached the coast at last it was battered with storms. A farmer gave them his barn for shelter, and they remained there many cold and weary weeks. But at last the winds subsided. A great stillness and frost settled over the land. The sea was dark but flat, and in these conditions they found a ship at last that was willing to make the crossing.

"God willing, we shall land on the coast of Kent," Augustine told them on the night before they set sail. "That land, which the South Saxons claim as their own, is ruled by King Ethelbert. This much we know certainly."

"Is this king a pagan ruler, Father?"

"He is a pagan ruler. But his wife is Christian. She is the daughter of the Frankish king, who gave her to Ethelbert only on condition that she might practice her faith. To this end he sent her Bishop

Liuthard for chaplain. We shall have allies in the war
we are to wage."

The brethren were silent, considering the little they
knew about the future. The journey had been hard,
but since Augustine had returned to them with the
Pope's letter they had never faltered. But a pagan king
must have pagan followers, and no one among the
brethren had any illusions that night about what might
greet them in Kent.

"Now let it be known," said Augustine, "that from
the time of our safe landing, Brother Sylvanus will
have his place at my side. For he is of English blood
and the language we shall hear is his language. And I
will have Wolfstan, his fellow countryman, to be my
bodyguard. These two shall be our interpreters. And I
earnestly pray that those of you who have already a
little knowledge, and those to whom God has granted
the gift of tongues, to learn quickly, for we and the
people must understand one another."

Brother Adrian the cook raised his hand.

"Have I your permission to speak, Father Abbot?"

"Speak, my son."

"There is also this young lad, Wolfstan's son, who
has this language. I ask that he may be my help in
finding provisions to feed us all. We shall need a
bargainer."

"Well, God will provide as always, Brother Adrian.
But let the boy be your helper. Almighty God never
despises a willing instrument, that is sure."

At this some of the monks murmured together.
Some smiled, but others frowned. Wolf, turning red-

der every second, looked at Brother Adrian for encouragement, for here was a firm friend.

Augustine called the boy over to him.

"Wolf, son of Wolfstan the Englishman, do you accept the charge I lay upon you in God's name?"

It was not much more than the third time Abbot Augustine had spoken directly to Wolf. The manner of his address now was solemn enough to make the boy stammer slightly when he replied, "I do, Father."

"Then you are as much a part of this holy mission as any one of us. . . . It is time to pray for a fair wind and a calm sea. God willing, tomorrow we sail for England."

As they drew near the unknown land a great silence fell upon those in the boat. Seeking a wind, they had sailed many miles close to the coast, then lain at anchor all one cold night. Morning brought the breeze and they veered into the open channel. Now the sun shone brilliantly on the cliff line ahead, so that the land seemed outlined in dazzling white. Above the cliffs a strip of greensward quickly lost itself in rolling forest, the trees stripped by winter. Great clouds—white cumulus piled up and rolling—moved fast over a sky that was blue, not as these men from southern Europe knew it, but with a pale northern clarity.

Augustine stood in the prow. Close by were Wolfstan, Brother Sylvanus, and Wolf. For the Abbot the land was a place of infinite promise where untold numbers of souls awaited the word he was bringing them. For Brother Sylvanus it was different. What he experienced then he shared with Wolfstan. He turned impulsively to his fellow countryman; and for the first time since he became a monk his face was the face of Eobald, less a chieftain's son than a poor captive sold into slavery. He put his hand on Wolfstan's arm and pressed it warmly.

"Forgive me, Wolfstan. I had almost forgotten. I am remembering now."

Wolfstan smiled and gave a quick nod of understanding.

"And I am remembering, Brother. Look—the light is different—as clear but paler. The cliffs seem lower. Look, Wolf, my boy, there is your country. Years have passed. There will be many changes. Who knows what we shall find? But this is your country and mine—"

"And mine, Wolf," said Brother Sylvanus. "So we three are brothers."

Augustine called to the ship's master: "What part of the land is this? Are we coming into Kent?"

"Yes, Father. We are bound for the Isle of Thanet. There is a good harbor there, one the Romans made. They called it Rutupiae. It is little used now, but it will serve us."

Wolf tugged at his father's arm. "Was it here that we lived?"

"West. Many miles to the west from here. There is forest and iron that we smelted."

"Shall we go back to that very place?"

"Who knows? Be content. This soil is the soil we came from, no matter if it be east or west."

At this moment they rounded the headland and

saw the harbor before them. The water seemed to smooth itself for their passage. They ran steadily before the breeze and made for their mooring. No other shipping was in sight. There was no sign of people, curious or hostile or welcoming. The great shingly beach curved to the north of them, and about the core of the harbor were many great buildings, some solid and enduring, some half derelict, many already fallen into heaps of stone.

The master took his ship beyond the harbor proper and anchored in shallow water on a sheltered beach. The monks girded up their gowns and prepared to wade to shore. Wolfstan would have carried Abbot Augustine, but he preferred to enter the country as humbly as the rest. As they reached the shore the monks one by one fell upon their knees and thanked God for their safety. The sailors and the servants, ordered by Wolfstan and aided by an eager Wolf, stood to make a chain through the shallows and toss the stores from hand to hand till they began to pile up on the shore. Last of all and most carefully handled was the solid chest that held within it those books upon which a nation's faith should be built: the Bible in two great volumes, a Book of the Gospels and a Psalter, a book that told of the early martyrs and a book of the Lives of the Apostles, together with various commentaries and expositions by learned men of certain chosen Epistles and Gospels.

This great box being delivered to Augustine, he laid his hands upon it and blessed it with special fervor.

For it was the only tangible and practical evidence of the faith the missionaries held within themselves.

When the last store was ashore and the last of the mission had waded to land, the ship's master asked for his money. As it was counted into his hand he kept looking uneasily about him, and he was so eager to be away that he made no attempt to bargain.

"We dare not miss the tide," he excused himself.

But his furtive glances suggested rather some fear of his surroundings. When the ship pulled up her anchor and sailed away on the instant, the missionaries gathered instinctively round their leader. For now indeed they were committed utterly. They were alone and unprotected in a land that might prove hostile. They had no shelter for the night and no certainty as to which way they should turn.

First, therefore, they gathered close together for their own comfort and sang *Te Deum* and the office of the hour, knowing that thus they would clear their minds and be strengthened for the task ahead.

Wolf, whose whole life at home had been bounded by such sounds as this—singing from the priory chapel as he was at his lessons, bells from the priory ringing him awake each morning, prayers framing and containing his day—even so found something strange and exalting in the chanting as it rang out, a little waveringly at first, over the empty beach. He stooped and picked up a handful of small pebbles, rubbing them between his fingers. In this way he seemed to make some contact with the new country that was yet so old in his imagination that it spoke to him of the very day he was born. He let the stones trickle from his hand, all save the smoothest and flattest, which he fitted into his left palm. It was a kind of talisman which would be frowned on, no doubt, by Abbot Augustine. But for Wolf it signified the beginning of a new life.

Without quite thinking what he was doing, he moved away from the rest and began walking toward a thicket of trees and bushes a hundred yards or so up the shore. He wanted to look at more than sea and sand and stones, more than the ruins of buildings pillared and corniced as those he had seen in Rome. He wanted to see something that lived and grew out of the soil that had bred him.

He reached the thicket and mounted a little hillock. As he did so, he was aware of some slight movement away on his right. He stopped in his tracks and stood silent and breathless, listening so hard that he seemed to hear his own thoughts.

For a second or two there was nothing more. Then he heard it again. It was the small sound of a dislodged stone rolling away down some slope.

Wolf's heart pounded and thumped. He looked cautiously around him. Then he realized that he might himself have displaced the stone as he climbed up the hill.

Yet somehow the sound had not seemed to come from behind him. He peered this way and that among the bushes, half longing and half dreading to see whatever it was that had made the movement. Some small animal—or the first of his own kinsmen, watching him suspiciously from a secure hiding place and perhaps already planning the destruction of an invader?

Wolf waited and listened. Then he heard it again. This time he could place the sound. It was much nearer than he had supposed. Indeed, it must have been close by his shoulder, for as he looked upward he saw something that almost made him swallow his own heart.

He saw a pair of eyes watching him steadily from a dense thornbush set on the hillside above him.

V

Fritha

FOR A SECOND Wolf remained utterly still. Behind him across the beach he heard the monks still chanting. If he shouted for help, no one would hear. If he turned and ran he might get a spear in his back, or one of those deadly small throwing knives his father had told him about. He waited helplessly, not knowing what to do.

The eyes stared from the bush and Wolf stared back. He stared so hard and so fiercely that suddenly the other eyes blinked. Once that had happened, they glanced away uneasily. The lashes fluttered with a kind of nervousness. Wolf began to grin. His heart stopped hammering and he relaxed. He scrambled up the remaining few yards toward the bush.

At once there was a scurry. The eyes vanished. The bush rocked and waved as someone began to struggle out of hiding. Wolf had an impression of waving arms and flying feet. He easily overtook them and pounced. There was a strangled cry and he snapped in a menacing, conqueror's voice, "Be silent!"

His captive squirmed and twisted and gasped but made no attempt to call out again. Still holding on to wrists that tugged vainly in his grip, Wolf overbalanced and fell on his knees. But he still hung on and in a second they were both on the ground.

Then the prisoner began to cry.

"Be silent!" Wolf said again. But he could not help grinning. There was not much glory in overcoming a girl no bigger than himself, but it was a relief not to have to deal with one of her older brothers, or perhaps her father. He still hung on because there was something about her crying that he did not entirely trust. He could see no tears. When Ana cried without tears it was always because she wanted to trick him. "How art thou named?" he demanded.

The crying ceased. She frowned. She wriggled back so that she was sitting on her heels and stared at him in a puzzled fashion.

"How art thou named?" He sounded impatient, and indeed he felt impatient—impatient and slightly worried. "Come, speak, girl, lest I strike thee."

To his fury, she burst out laughing. He let her hands go as though she had spat at him. He was now more than merely worried, he was utterly bewildered.

"Why dost thou seem so mirthful, girl?"

At which she covered her face with her hands and collapsed into convulsive giggles.

Wolf felt helpless and angry. She was a skinny little thing with hair so fair it was almost white, and it could do with a combing, he thought. In spite of the manner of their meeting and her mockery now, she was somehow not at all unfriendly. But what was he to do if she would not answer when he spoke to her, if she merely burst out laughing at the very sound of his voice? He tried *Be silent!* again, for she had seemed to understand that. She still did so, for she stifled her laughter. But she had lost her awe of him, that much was clear. For a glorious moment at the very beginning he had been a conqueror. Now he was quite clearly almost an equal. If things went on at this rate he would soon be her inferior. He stared at her silently, afraid to open his mouth.

He decided he would have to take her to his father and Brother Sylvanus and see if they could make her listen to plain sense. It was very disheartening for him, the first time he spoke his own tongue in his own country to his own countrywoman to meet with nothing but mocking laughter.

He rose. He did his best to look and sound commanding. "Come."

She hesitated a second, then scrambled to her feet. She understood that word, which was something. Perhaps she was a little lacking in wits and only understood very simple words? He did not believe it—she looked very far from witless to him. He reached out and took her hand, and she allowed him to do so. But when he moved off, leading her, she hesitated.

"Come!" He was growing impatient. He held on to her hard, but this was a mistake, for she began to struggle. She scratched at his wrist with her free hand, but he managed to get her away from the shelter of the bushes and out on the slope, from which they could see the monks gathered in a little crowd with their supplies about them. Wolf pointed, and the girl looked across the beach in silence, and perhaps fear, for she tried to wriggle free. "Behold!" Wolf pointed again. "Behold where noble men pray to their God."

At that, in spite of her struggles, she gave the loudest laugh of all and nearly fell down again, she was so doubled up with mirth.

He was so annoyed that he let her go. He could no longer be bothered with her. He turned his back and swung off across the shore. As he went he heard a man's voice calling.

"Fritha!" He was somewhere out of sight. "Where are you, Fritha? Daughter!"

Wolf swung round. The girl was still staring after him. She made a face at him, then turned on her heel, calling as she went:

"Here! Coming! Coming, Father."

And she ran off and disappeared over the rising ground. Almost immediately she reappeared with a man beside her and pointed excitedly down the beach.

Wolf was more puzzled than ever. The man had called and she had answered in the language he knew to be his own. Certainly she had answered briefly, ungracefully perhaps. But if he understood her, why should she not understand him? Feeling thoroughly baffled, Wolf rejoined the monks.

Wolfstan looked up sharply as the boy approached.

"Where have you been? Do not leave the rest till we know more. It is too quiet here—it is not natural. Perhaps they are arming themselves."

"What are we to do now, Father?" Wolf saw that the stores were being taken up and the monks were moving off across the shingle.

"We shall make camp for the night. Brother Sylvanus will go with letters to the King."

"Does he know the way?"

"He will ask it," replied Wolfstan shortly.

Wolf was aware that his father was worried, but none the less he could not help smiling, for he had a quick vision of Brother Sylvanus courteously inquiring the way of some peasant and being greeted with gales of laughter.

"Father, just now something very strange happened to me—"

Wolf got no further, for there was a sudden commotion among the monks, who were pointing and exclaiming in great agitation. Across the beach came the man Wolf had already seen, accompanied by half a dozen more. They carried thick wooden staves. Behind them, on the skyline, could be seen an assortment of people, men and women and children, of all ages and sizes.

Augustine moved at once to the head of his brethren and stood waiting. He held his hands at his sides, that all might see he carried no weapon. He called to the rest to do the same.

"Brother Sylvanus, stand by me to be my interpreter. Wolfstan! These are your own blood. Speak to them."

Wolfstan stepped ahead of the rest. He called out to the approaching men, "We are all friends. I greet my countrymen."

Wolf almost put his fingers in his ears so that he would not hear the laughter that must surely come. But nothing happened. The first man, whom the girl had called father, stepped a pace or two forward in his turn.

"Where is your ship?"

"Sailed home again. We only are left here on this shore. Tell us where we may shelter."

The man looked from Wolfstan to Augustine and back again.

"Who is your leader?"

Brother Sylvanus at once stepped forward. He had a good rich voice and it rang confidently.

"Hearest thou, friends? Behold our leader, who comes with tidings of great joy. When thou hearest him—"

He broke off, for the men looked from one to the other among themselves, and smiled, then half laughed and stifled the laughter as well as they could.

"Are you kings?" demanded the first man, still smiling into his beard. "Only kings speak thus. Only kings long dead." And now he laughed out loud.

"Nay, friend," began Brother Sylvanus, trying not to frown.

Wolfstan broke in without apology. "No," he said. "Not kings. But they have a message from the King of Kings. And they seek your King Ethelbert, who must hear it before any one of you."

The six men stopped laughing and conferred together. At last their leader spoke again.

"I am Cyneog. I am a farmer like all these here. If you seek the King you seem to come in peace. Let him be judge of that. There is a good yard where you can shelter. Send to the King and stay here guarded until his answer comes."

Wolfstan then interpreted this to Augustine, who nodded his agreement. With Wolfstan constantly acting as go-between, the monks took up the stores and other supplies, and the coffer with the holy books, and set off behind Cyneog.

At the tail of the procession Wolf, with a sack of meal on his shoulders, tagged along frowning. He could not understand why his father was able to talk to Cyneog and the others, while Brother Sylvanus—and his best pupil, whose style had been much praised— were met with outbursts of laughter.

Suddenly he found someone walking a little way behind him. He looked over his shoulder and saw the fair-haired girl.

"I am Fritha. You?"

"Wolf." If she could only manage words of one syllable he had better reply in the same way. But the matter nagged at him. "Why *kings?*" he demanded. "Why *long dead kings?*"

"It is in the songs. The bards sing tales of kings who speak so. But they are dead—all dead." And she imitated him, giggling as she did so, "*How art thou named?*"

The explanation began to struggle through Wolf's confusion of mind. Brother Sylvanus, when he was Eobald, had been a chieftain's son. He had never spoken in Wolfstan's blunt rough way. Wolfstan had been pleased, when Wolf went to learn from Brother Sylvanus, to hear this grander speech. But Wolf's lessons had been based on the poems and songs and legends that Brother Sylvanus remembered hearing sung and told by the bards in his father's hall. Gradually, in the years during which he had heard no other of his own countrymen, Brother Sylvanus had fallen entirely into the old poetic way of speech, the speech of *long dead kings*, as Cyneog had said, handing Wolf as it were the key to the mystery.

A great deal must be unlearned, Wolf realized. He told himself soberly he would have to keep his wits about him. It was not at all pleasant to be laughed at, least of all by a towheaded girl.

"Show me the way," he commanded, for the rest
had vanished while he stopped to talk. "Come on—
make haste."

Fritha smiled. "It is better when you are a boy and
not a dead king. . . . This way, Wolf."

And she ran skippingly ahead of him. Her fair
hair danced on her shoulders, but it was still dread-
fully rough and tangled. Once Wolf had made his
mother a comb out of bone for a present. It was
possible he might do as much for Fritha if she be-
haved herself and did not laugh at him any more.

In the camp they made within the farmer's stockade, Wolf as usual helped Brother Adrian with the
cooking. But that was not his only task. His father
had gone with Brother Sylvanus, once the language
difficulty was realized, and Wolf was thus the only
one in the camp who could speak with any fluency
to the English. This he did carefully but with increasing success. Certainly it was much easier, if uglier,
than what he had learned from Brother Sylvanus during the years in Rome. He was beginning almost to
chatter with Fritha. Now that she had stopped laughing, she was helpful and kind. He could tell her about
Ana and know she would listen. And because she too
had no mother—though it was many years since her
death—they were much in sympathy. He told her how
his father had been taken and put up for sale in the
Roman market place, and how Pope Gregory had given
him his freedom. And he told her about Rome and
the way life went there, till her eyes were round with

astonishment. Wolf suspected she had had little idea
that any other places existed beyond the shore on the
south, the forest and hills to north and east and west.
But she knew where the King lived.

"He lives in Canterbur'."

"*Where?*" Wolf frowned. "It is called Cantiacorum—
Durovernum Cantiacorum—that's its full name."

"Now you are talking like an old man again."

"First a dead king, now an old man."

"Well, the old men call it Cantia—What you said."

"That was what the Romans called it."

"Who?"

"The Romans, stupid. Haven't you ever heard of
them? The Romans from Rome. Where my home was.
Where Ana is still. Three hundred years they lived here
and looked after the place and built great buildings."

And if they had not had to go because of troubles
in their own country, he thought, invaders would not
have come and destroyed the cities and the faith that
had been brought to the people.

"They're not here now," said Fritha, dismissing the
Romans. "Only us. The country is our country."

Wolf was torn in two. He had been so sure he
was every inch of him a native of this country. Yet
Fritha had only to speak lightly of the Romans for
him to bristle into defense. It was almost a relief to
end the conflict by answering Brother Adrian's call
to help with the breadmaking.

It was not many miles from the coast to the King's
palace at Cantiacorum—or must it be Canterbury or

Cantuar, as they now heard it called? When two days passed and the deputies did not return, the brethren grew very uneasy.

"They have been set upon and murdered, mark my word."

"The King mistrusts them and is questioning them."

"Or he has thrown them into prison."

"Or he delights in disputing with them and will not let them go."

"Father Abbot, what if we are all to be made martyrs before our message is given?"

"God's will be done, my children. But I know it is not so." He spoke not presumptuously, but in the confidence of his own great faith.

It was on the third day that one of the youngest monks cried out that he saw a cavalcade approaching. Everyone crowded to where he was standing on rising ground, from which they could look toward the northeast above the stockade. There sure enough was the dust of cantering horses, and they soon saw that ten or a dozen riders were approaching. It was impossible, however, to make out if these were the returning messengers joined with some others, or a band of fighting men coming to take the invaders by force.

"I can see Brother Sylvanus' robes!" cried the young monk whose sight was so good.

Wolf pushed to his side.

"Do you see my father also?"

"He could be any one of ten and more. This cold wind makes my eyes water. There, I can see no more."

Augustine now ordered that they leave the stockade, where only a pretense was made of guarding them, and go out in an orderly fashion to meet the cavalcade. A rough track wound from the farm up the hill. As they followed the track, they sang together, partly in piety, but partly to raise up their spirits, which were disturbed by the unknown.

Wolf followed after the procession at a little distance. He saw that as they sang together the monks were strengthened until their community was like a building with stout walls. From the windows of this building there seemed to shine forth many lights, for their faith was radiant, even if their human courage sometimes failed a little.

As the procession reached the brow of the hill, the cavalcade was seen near at hand. Wolf forgot his manners and thrust past the file of singing brethren, intent only on finding his father.

Someone caught him by the shoulder. To his horror he found himself looking up into the stern face of the Father Abbot.

"Wait," said Augustine. "Do you not see the cross-bearer? A man of God is approaching. It is likely to be Bishop Liuthard. The Queen's own chaplain has come to give us welcome. Keep your place, my child."

Red in the face, Wolf dropped back again. And even when he saw Wolfstan safe and well he managed to stay patiently where he was. He saw Brother Sylvanus, his face shining with content, hurry toward Augustine, then lead him to the head of the cavalcade.

It was indeed the Queen's chaplain who had come to welcome Augustine to the kingdom of Kent.

"I am to greet you from the King, Father Abbot. And from Queen Bertha, our most Christian lady. And I am to say this—that King Ethelbert has heard your message and respects it. Within a few days he will come himself to this Isle of Thanet and speak with you."

"Now God be praised, my lord," said Augustine.

"But I am to say that the meeting must be in some open place."

At this there was a confused murmur among the gathering about Augustine. But he remained calm.

"As the King pleases, my lord Bishop."

"Father," said Liuthard, "this is a pagan land and the King is bound to respect his own fears. It is thought by his advisers that you may seek to work some magic on him. But this, by ancient superstition, you may not do so long as you do not meet beneath any roof."

"May God enlighten him," said Augustine.

Behind him a slow silence settled over the listening monks. Indeed they were likely to enter upon a hard task in this barbaric place.

VI

The King of Kent

THE SIGHT of Bishop Liuthard had greatly impressed Cyneog and many of his fellow farmers. Most people living in those parts had heard that the Queen followed a faith different from their own, and different, therefore, from the King's. They knew, too, from old stories only partly understood, that this faith had been practiced in the past in other parts

79

of Britain. Some knew from travelers' tales that in the West—in Wales, in Cornwall and across the sea in Ireland—there were Christian bishops ministering to large communities. Why or how this should be they made no effort to understand. The people of those distant parts of the country were Celts, members of the ancient race which once had been spread throughout the land. Of them it was true as in the old song sung by many bards: *"Their God they shall praise, Their language they shall keep. Their land they shall lose. . . ."*

But Cyneog and his fellows in the Kentish countryside were like their counterparts in other such communities. They were simple people concerned with simple things. The necessities of life were what they strove for and the striving kept them busy. With sowing and harvest, hunting and fishing, with dragging iron and salt from the reluctant earth, with bringing up their families and being ever on the alert against enemies, they had not much time for the refinements of life, of which religion was the most obvious. True, they did not neglect the old gods and accepted their seasonal demands for sacrifice. Those who lived in the ruins of cities and villas built during the Roman occupation, worshiped at the altars of battered temples. But for Cyneog and his fellows the rule was simpler. Their places of worship were wooded groves where Yggdrasill, the tree god, might be found in a single ash growing strongly among oak. Thus they were loyal to Woden and his kin, who had planted the mightiest tree, the great ash whose roots they believed, held the world together.

In spite of this, though they were cautious, the people of Thanet for the most part were friendly to the missionaries. It had not been such a bad thing, perhaps, that those first exchanges on the seashore had broken down in laughter. And when it became known that the King would come in person to speak with Augustine, the people felt proud that they had cared for him and his fellows instead of thrusting them back into the sea, as they might have done.

There were the inevitable few who dissented from the general opinion. Of these the loudest was Hardra, a man taller than most of these English, and therefore by sheer physical presence a leader. He was Fritha's uncle, her dead mother's brother. He was a man who smiled very seldom, and every man attached to the mission knew that he could be dangerous.

Although Wolf had his share of the work, he also had a good deal of time to himself. It was far more than he was accustomed to. Whenever he found himself free, he would look around for Fritha. Though he never said to her *be at such-and-such a place,* he was almost certain to find her somewhere near at hand. She would be sitting idly on the stone wall near the cattle trough if the weather was dry. Or feeding the geese by the pond, or driving the pigs in, or any one of a dozen small activities which she performed casually, without complaint but without much interest, either. She was not like the other girls Wolf saw about the farms and holdings, for they seemed to toil ceaselessly. Their fathers shouted at them, their brothers bullied them, they were like little slaves in the family. But Fritha was her father's only child, and since her mother's death she was everything in life that he cherished.

"When the King comes here, Wolf," she said, "will the Queen come too?"

"Who can tell? As she is a Christian, then she might come. As a woman who can have no place in the councils of men, then she may not."

"Oh, I do wish she might come! I have never yet in all my life seen a lady. They say kings and queens wear circlets of gold on their heads, and jewels in their ears and on their fingers, and great brooches on their cloaks. Is it true?"

"I should judge it to be true." Wolf knew very little more than Fritha about kings and queens. But he told her about the Roman ladies, in their light veils that blew in the wind, veils so fine that it was possible to see through them to the gold braids and pins the ladies wore in their hair. "As though they were decked out in stars."

"Like the Queen of the Fairies!" Fritha cried in delight.

Wolf looked at her sternly. She was a shocking little pagan. "Like Our Lady in Heaven," he corrected her.

"Oh, but my uncle Hardra is cousin to a Druid,

and *he* says the Queen of the Fairies wears a golden crown. And Signa, his daughter, has seen her. And so has her brother Uthdra."

"Your uncle Hardra is no friend to Father Augustine. And if a Druid is what I think—a sort of priest—then no wonder. But one day soon there will be no more Druids in all the land."

"They will not go because you say so!"

"Not because *I* say so." Wolf swallowed his annoyance and was silent, suddenly aware that he was not by a long way clever enough to argue the case. "Any one of the brothers could explain, Fritha." And lamely changing the subject he asked, "Is Uthdra that great lout with black hair and a broken nose—the one who was hauling wood this morning?"

"His nose was broken in fair fight."

"That does not make him any handsomer."

Fritha plaited her fingers together across her knee and did not look at Wolf as she replied. "Well, I must get used to his broken nose, handsome or no, for he will be my husband one day."

Indignation made Wolf stutter. "Th-that fellow? Would you choose him?"

"Of course I wouldn't. But what girl can choose her husband? It was arranged by our parents before either of us was old enough to speak."

"But he is your cousin, Fritha. You cannot marry your cousin. It is not allowed."

"Not allowed? Who will not allow it, if my father wants it—and my uncle too?"

"Well, you could not if you were a Christian. The Church would not allow it."

Fritha burst out laughing. "If your Church is strong enough to stop my father doing as he wants, then it is certainly powerful!"

"You don't understand—"

"No, Wolf! I cannot understand at all why your Abbot Augustine should decide whom I may marry!"

Wolf had once listened to the oldest monk in the Priory, Father Antoninus, explaining to a young novice exactly how strong and sure was the authority of the Church in such matters as this. He wished he could remember the right words now. But all his memory offered him was the patient gentleness of the old man as he went over and over the matter for the novice, who was not very clever.

"If you were a Christian," Wolf began again. Then he stopped. He had been going to say something rather shocking. He blushed inwardly. He had thought, in one blinding moment, that if he could only explain properly about all this Fritha could not fail to see the advantages of becoming a Christian and he, the youngest and humblest of them all, might thus carry home the first convert. This was dreadful. It was dishonest and vain and insulting to the faith itself. It was what Brother Severus called "the right rhyme with the wrong reason." None the less, Wolf could not get the idea of Fritha as Uthdra's wife settled at all comfortably in his mind. There must be some honest way of dealing with this business. Perhaps her father's heart would be moved when he heard Augustine preach, or perhaps Uthdra himself might be converted. But somehow Wolf liked that idea less.

He kicked viciously at a stone lying by his foot. It went skimming across the beach where they had been idling along behind Cyneog's two cows as they grazed on what green they could find. The stone went as far as a fishing boat that had just been hauled onto the beach with its catch.

If Wolf had been strong enough and clever enough, he would have liked to put Fritha into the boat and sail away with her to some far coast where Uthdra would never have the power to find her.

The King did not come to Thanet as he had promised, in a few days, nor in a week. There was news that he had gone off on a mission to the far ends of his realm, which stretched in the northeast to the borders of the kingdom of Northumbria. The missionaries were obliged to remain where they were, not wanting in any way to offend the King by preaching their faith among the people until permission had been given.

Because of this, there was murmuring on all sides. The monks were eager to begin their mission. The local people were beginning to find their hospitality overstrained. Hardra's voice was now heard increasingly.

"Who are they? How do we know that they are not warlocks come to destroy us? Truly the Queen's own Bishop came to speak with them. And the King was coming. But the King has not come. He has not come because of wise counsel, no doubt—some revelation from the gods. Why do we keep these men here with us? We had best be rid of them."

Wolfstan was all for sending to the Queen, but Augustine would not be moved.

"Patience," was all he would say.

This was the early part of the year. They had been waiting, uncertain and increasingly fearful, for many weeks when word came at last.

That morning they had wakened to a great change. Spring had come while they slept. The air was suddenly soft and the sea had lost its winter color. Beyond the farm enclosure, the circle of the village, where the trees began there was a kind of bloom, a mist of change that would become the green of unfolding leaves. The birds were alert. Overnight doubt had become expectation.

And indeed the monks had barely finished the first office of the day when a horseman came riding at speed over the hill and bore down toward the coast. Away on his left the sun was lighting the ruins of the old port. And the sun shone too on Augustine's face, as he lifted it toward the northeast.

"Word is coming from the King. At last. May this day see the beginning of our ministration."

The monks gathered about him. One thing was certain; today they would be either rejected or accepted. If rejected, what would become of them? Would they be allowed to depart peacefully, or would they face martyrdom?

The messenger reined in within a few yards of Augustine. He called out something that Brother Sylvanus quickly translated.

"It is a greeting, Father. Uncouth, but a greeting. The King is conscious of the delay but he has been about his land, pacifying and counseling. He sends a delayed word of welcome."

"Thank him, Brother. Ask where the King will speak to us, and when."

Brother Sylvanus had learned by now to discard his archaic speech and use a freer style.

"Does the King intend to come here to conference?"

"Yes, to Thanet. He is already approaching from the mainland. He will come to counsel at noon. In the oak grove above the eastern shore. At noon. At high noon, neither sooner nor later."

And with this thrice-repeated instruction, the messenger turned and rode away. He gave a brief signal with his raised hand, but whether it was a salute meaning farewell, or an ill-concealed sign against the evil eye, it was difficult to tell.

A faint smile moved over Augustine's stern face.

"Not only the King fears enchantment, Brothers. But the Queen will intercede for us. Bishop Liuthard has had gentle treatment through her, and so shall we. If the King had been truly paganhearted, would he have kept his word that his Queen should freely practice her own faith?"

They had argued this among themselves so often that no one replied to it now. As Augustine looked round his flock he must have seen a score of varying expressions to encourage or discourage him. That brother might not be strong enough, that brother would die willingly, that brother is a plodder and will be cheerful either way. . . . God would be with them, but he had after all created them men, not saints, and as men they must live or die.

Within seconds of the messenger's departure, word had gone round that the King was on his way. Though his business was with Abbot Augustine, there was no man within miles who would not leave what he was doing and hurry to greet the King.

If it had been possible to stand upon some pinnacle in the center of that countryside, it would have been possible, too, to see people moving from every shore of the island toward one focal point. It was as though word of the King's coming had been trumpeted in all the corners of the island. The people were on the move from every farm and every settlement. It was said there were six hundred families dwelling in the island and not one seemed to have stayed at home. They were families of all kinds and sizes. Sometimes a father carried two small children on his shoulder while half a dozen more followed behind, with the wife helping along the old parents. Sometimes a young husband and wife took turns to carry their first child, still in swaddling clothes. Often an aged grandparent was trundled in a handcart. Not only from the farms, but from the ruins of the harbor town they were pouring. These last were ragged and filthy, men and women who had dug themselves holes to live in among the dead homes built by men now departed, rather than have the labor of making a place of their own. They scraped some sort of a living, their children were half starved and were covered with sores from rat bites, for the ruins swarmed with vermin.

These were not the only ones who came from the town. On the slopes above the harbor, prosperous Roman merchants had built themselves villas of great comfort and solidity. Many of these remained still in good repair, and there dwelt those men who knew how to make a living out of the miseries of others. They had formed themselves into some sort of council and administered the broken town to their own gain and satisfaction. They, too, with horses to carry them and serfs in attendance, rode out to greet King Ethelbert on this visitation. They added color to the crowd, for often their tunics and mantles were dyed a splendid red, a scarlet dye which came from a cockle harvested on the shore. It was said that the sun could not fade this color, but rather it grew more beautiful with age.

Since Cyneog and Hardra and the rest were soon making for the appointed meeting place, it was easy for Wolf to join them, moving at once to Fritha's side. There was no sign of Uthdra. He must have been about somewhere, and Wolf was constantly looking out for him, anticipating trouble if he arrived and found Fritha with a companion. And indeed very soon, though Uthdra himself did not appear, his mother, Eswige, called Fritha to come and walk by her side.

Wolf fell back a little. But he looked constantly toward Fritha, and she toward him, grimacing when Eswige was not looking. Fritha had taken care with her appearance for once. Her face and hands were scrubbed until they shone and she had got the tangles out of her hair; it hung softly on her shoulders, looking less white than a fine pale gold as the sun caught it. It would be terrible, he thought, when she was grown old enough to be obliged to cover her hair, as all the women did, wrapping a cloth over it and round their necks so that, at times, they looked like bundles of rag.

Now up at the head of what had become a straggling procession, the monks who bore their great cross before Augustine, and a banner on which was wrought in colors the image of Our Lord, began to sing and chant together. For this was the simplest way of praying together that man might devise. Not all who entered the order were clever enough to learn prayers invented for them by the learned. But if there were some who found the words of the psalms obscure, the warmth of their upraised voices made up for that, and the sound of their singing rose and swelled in splendor and strength as they neared the appointed meeting place.

By the time the procession of monks and the people from the shore reached the place, there was already a good crowd there. There was constant movement as kinsfolk and friends found and greeted one another. It was almost like a fair day, Wolf thought. And he wondered how Tullus had managed in the juggling last

summer. It was so long ago he must be practicing for
the next one by this time.

There was a broad grassy ride among the oak trees
to north and west of the little plain. When Abbot Augustine reached the plain, he led his monks forward
and across the open ground, then turned and faced
toward the ride, for it was certain the King must come
that way to the meeting.

The day which had begun with such promise continued fair. A gentle sun shone from a bland sky. As
their elders fell deeper into expectant gossip, the children began to race about, to shout together and tum-
ble on the grass. It was easy, in the midst of all this,
for Fritha to leave her aunt and slip back to Wolf.

"Will the King come soon, Wolf?" She seized his
hand in her excitement.

"The messenger said it would be at noon exactly."
Wolf stared up at the sky, sliding his hand out of
Fritha's with the excuse that he needed to shield his
eyes from the sun. If they stood hand in hand in that
crowd, someone would be sure to point at them. For
they must appear either as a pair of simple babies,
or else as grown people who have chosen one another—and they were neither one nor the other.

"Listen!"

Far away there was the sound of a horn. Everyone
there heard it. The chattering ceased. A wave of excitement ran over the crowd. Then they shouted:

"It is the King! Our King is coming! The King!
The King!"

And they ran toward the mouth of the ride, each

one wanting to be the first to raise the cry that the King was in sight. A high babble of feverish anticipation took the place of the easy gossiping. How would he be attended? How would he look? Some said he was fair, but others said he was black as pitch in hair and beard and had fierce thick eyebrows. And would the Queen come too? And if the Queen why not their children, the young Princes? So it went on until the horn sounded a second time, nearer, much nearer, so near that the harshly beautiful sound made Wolf shiver, and this time it was he who caught Fritha's hand.

"Look!" she cried. "Oh, look—look!"

At the far end of the broad ride, where it curved away among the trees, the first horseman had come into view. There was a light mist in among the tall trees where the sun did not penetrate, and the men on horseback seemed to materialize from the mist— first one, then four, then ten, then a great crowd of them approaching at an easy canter. They were men at arms and warriors whose exploits gave them a place beside the King. They rode sturdy little horses, heavy in the neck and shoulder.

"There he is!"

One man rode alone among the rest. Everything about him proclaimed his identity—his richer clothes, his finer horse, his haughty, confident bearing. He rode without looking to left or right, imperious and straight-backed.

Now the ride was full of men and horses and the ground shook with the thud of hooves. The people

waiting dragged their caps off and knelt, or even
bowed their heads against the ground at the approach
of their master. He had power of life and death over
every one of them and they accepted this authority
without question. If he pointed his finger at one of
them and said *Kill me that man,* then most assuredly
it would be done. Yet it was not in fear that they
greeted him, but in unquestioning loyalty. They be-
longed to him. They were ready to serve him. And
none knew why this should be, save that it was what
they had been born to, and their fathers before them.

At last there was none standing in all that gathering save Augustine and the monks gathered behind him. Fritha had tugged Wolf down beside her
so sharply that he almost fell on his nose. He half
struggled to his feet, then went down on his knee
again. For this King was his King, as well as hers,
and something in his blood was moved by the same
submissive loyalty as all the rest.

A hundred paces from Augustine, the King halted
and all his followers closed in about him. They seemed
to make a shield, as though to protect him. At that
Wolf realized a strange thing—it was simply that the
stranger, Augustine, standing upright there with the
cross borne at his shoulder, supported by a few unarmed men, was none the less stronger than Ethelbert,
King of Kent, on whose hospitality and understanding
he depended. If anyone there was afraid, it was not
Augustine and the brethren, facing possible death—it
was the King and his court. For what they feared was
the sharpest fear of all—the fear of the unknown.

Fritha suddenly gripped Wolf's hand so hard that he gasped. She was looking past the King, back along the ride among the trees. Wolf turned to look and saw that a second cavalcade was entering what now seemed almost an arena.

"Is it—? Oh it is, it is! The Queen!"

She was riding a gray palfrey and she wore a white flowing veil—held to her head by a thin golden circlet, then twisting around her neck and over her shoulders. Behind her rode two of her ladies, and men at arms. But at her side was Bishop Liuthard.

The Queen rode into the green open space, and when she came within a suitable distance she bowed to the King, her husband.

But then, instead of joining him close at his side, she moved on a few paces. Then she reined in her horse and called to an attendant, who ran to the animal's head and held the rein. Then another attendant helped her to the ground.

"The grass is so wet," murmured Fritha, who was herself kneeling in it quite cheerfully, "her feet will be soaked."

Undisturbed by the wet grass, the Queen advanced toward Augustine. She moved gently, steadily, without hurry. Suddenly they saw her sink down on her knees.

An extraordinary sound came from the crowd. It began as a murmur, then swelled until it was almost a groan. There was shock in it, and disapproval, and there was fear. There was admiration, too, for the grace and humility of the Queen's bowed head and folded hands.

The King made a sharp movement forward, then checked and held up his hand, for his followers had moved instantly and one had his dagger in his hand.

To many of them there it could only seem as though their Queen knelt before a god of her own. Since it was known among most of them that their gods were not hers, they could only conclude that a strange god stood before them.

Some covered their faces instantly, others drew their children close, laying one hand across their eyes and with the other making the sign against evil.

Augustine, deeply moved by the Queen's gesture, put out both his hands to raise her up.

But it was she who took his hand and kissed it.

Behind the King the ranks of his followers grew increasingly restive. But still he held them in check, and with them all the rest of the great crowd.

Aware of the tension, dangerously gathering, Bishop Liuthard dismounted and moved to join the Queen.

Behind Wolf and Fritha someone said, "He is the High Priest of the Queen's god."

"Then does he come to make sacrifice to the god?"

Within seconds the word *sacrifice* had sighed itself over the assembly, changing as it went into something menacing and terrible.

"The High Priest will sacrifice the Queen!"

Someone screamed it out.

Startled, the King turned his head, his horse moved suddenly and he put down his hand to quiet it.

Instantly his followers answered what seemed to be a signal. The sun shone on drawn swords.

Brother Lucian was carrying the Cross. He was one of those who had learned a few words of the barbaric language spoken by these people, and he seemed to gain some idea of what might happen even before the King turned.

He raised up the Cross, and the sun caught it and turned it to fire. He moved forward, standing so that the Cross was like a great golden weapon upraised to protect those below and behind it.

This time the King dropped the reins on his horse's neck and held up both hands firmly and commandingly.

The impulsive movement forward of the men at arms, the chieftains and the crowd of peasants, was checked into a jostle that at last died away into stillness.

Augustine, stooping, raised the Queen to her feet. He spoke over his shoulder to Brother Sylvanus.

"Implore the Queen to take me to King Ethelbert."

Smiling as she listened, the Queen took Augustine once more by the hand, this time with the confiding gesture of a pupil toward a well-loved master.

"Stay quietly where you are," Augustine commanded the brethren.

Then he went forward with the Queen across the grass.

The King did not move. A pace or two ahead of him the Queen paused and spoke. Her voice was too soft for any who were at a distance to hear. But her message was seen in her smile, in her outstretched hand and the way she turned from one man to the other as though praying them to be friends.

Then Augustine, looking up toward the King on his horse, spoke clearly in words that only his followers and the Queen and Bishop Liuthard could understand.

"May the peace of Almighty God be with you—and in your heart—and in your hands—until the day when I shall sign you with the sign of the Cross and call you to His bidding."

In the intense silence that now held the crowd, the King swung out of the saddle. He went toward the Queen; he went within a pace of Augustine. For a second the two men stood looking into one another's eyes. Then, very briefly, the King touched Augustine on the shoulder. He spoke to him quietly and clearly.

"I have heard of your message and I do not fear it or your purpose. If this is your wish, come to my city and I will give you and yours a dwelling place. And in my city you may preach. The rest is for you."

Of all this, Augustine may have understood two words. But by the King's tone and his steady, shrewd look, and by the Queen's smile, he knew that the first danger was past.

VII

The Beginning

THAT ABBOT Augustine and his monks should be housed by the King's command in Canterbury, that he should give them the church of St. Martin, which had been the Queen's own chapel, in which to preach and pray, was so comforting to some of the brethren after their ordeals that they became quite puffed up. Here, surely, they decided, was a sign of God's especial favor. Divine Grace, they were assured, had moved the King's heart to kindness; and this indeed argued, they said, that their early faults, their timidity that must be called cowardice, had been forgiven. But on Good Friday, Augustine preached them such a sermon as none who heard it would ever forget. "*Watch and pray*" was his text, and its chastening message was very clear.

After that, even the most self-confident among them was ready to be humble. Every one of them prepared eagerly for the exacting work that now lay ahead.

Much of the work was practical. The church of St. Martin was in poor repair—it had been in disuse for many long years when the Queen came to Kent and took it for her own. Also, the lodging given by the King must be enlarged to hold the community. The King lent them masons and carpenters. He gave them land to till and sent farmers to help and advise on the ways of a soil and a climate so unlike what they had known. The King did not call for any account of the gifts he made, nor come to see how the building progressed, nor listen to the word that was preached by his consent. He had his large realm to administer, he was often away from his capital, and that was reason enough. In his absence, the Queen would sanction this or that improvement, commending the work of both monks and laymen and making herself in all things their benefactress.

Wolf and his father were lodged in the gatehouse

of the monastery, with two of the porters. They looked after themselves as they were accustomed. Wolf still helped Brother Adrian in the kitchen, though not all the time. He was most in demand when it came to bargaining with the local people. He always went to the market with Brother Adrian and Brother Leonardo, the butler. Also he was now able to work with his father about the administration of the land, to keep tally of grain and meal and arrange for such things as milling and the care of beasts being fattened for slaughter.

But with so much to do himself, with so much going on around him, he was often restless. He was homesick, he told himself. He realized with a renewed sadness that his mother was truly dead. And he missed Ana, from whom he had parted voluntarily. But for all his sorrows about his mother and his sister, what bothered him most of all was parting from Fritha. She had somehow made up to him for what he had left behind in Rome, and now she was left behind in her turn at her father's farm. Day after day he planned to walk to the coast and cross to the island to see her. But day after day he was kept busy and the opportunity did not come.

And then, one morning at the beginning of May, he went to the market with Brother Adrian and Brother Leonardo, and there was Cyneog driving in two fat sheep for sale, and Fritha walking beside him. She must have washed her hair, for it tossed as light as feathers on her shoulders.

Wolf dashed toward her, and then stopped. He

had not seen her for weeks—she might have forgotten him.

"Wolf!" Fritha's face lit up with pleasure and excitement, and she ran in her turn to meet him. "I knew we should find you if we came to Canterbur'!" Cyneog paused when he heard her voice. He looked at Wolf and gave him a quick, friendly nod. "How are things with you and the brothers, Wolf? You have been missed. Is your father well?"

"He is very well. Are these fat sheep for slaughter? Brother Adrian will be glad to look at them. He is there—with the swineherd. He'll call me to bargain in a moment."

Sure enough, Brother Adrian, a very determined expression on his thin dark face, was looking about him for help. He had chosen a sow and her ten piglets, and now the swineherd was haggling over the price. As Wolf went to answer Brother Adrian's appeal, he knew that Fritha was following. It gave him pleasure to conduct the business in a very forthright and efficient manner, knowing that she was watching and listening.

"I shall see you in sole charge of provisioning soon," Brother Adrian said. "But you'll have to take your vows first."

"Is Wolf to be a monk?" Fritha cried.

"No!" Wolf laughed, because the brothers were always slyly suggesting he might discover he had a vocation to become one of them in the service of God. He knew there had been dismay in Fritha's tone, and that made him want to laugh, too, just for sheer pleasure of her interest in him. Rather red in the face, he changed the subject. "Cyneog is here with two fine sheep, Brother Adrian. Will you see them?"

"Yes, show me. Here's Brother Leonardo, too. He's a better judge of sheep than I am."

Speaking in two languages gave Wolf a feeling of power and pleasure. He stood with the three men and they all listened to what he said.

"Cyneog says they have been fed on milk, Brother."

"Tell him that is as good a joke as any."

"Brother Leonardo doubts you, Cyneog."

"Doubts me, does he? Tell him it was from the second milking!"

"Cyneog says, Brother—"

And so it went on, until the bargain was made to the satisfaction of them all. This was a good day for Wolf—fine and sunny, with jobs well done at its very beginning and a meeting with Fritha to make it complete.

Two fat sheep meant not only meat, but also wool and mutton-fat for the salves made by Brother Paul, the infirmarian, and candles, too, which would be the everyday candles. The altar candles were made of finest wax.

The brothers and Cyneog fell into conversation, with Wolf as go-between. About them the bustle of the market continued. Then they said good-bye and Wolf and the two monks began to drive the sheep and the pigs back to the monastery. The piglets constantly became separated from their mother, whose fierceness was alarming, so Fritha came to chase the little ones back each time they strayed. Then Cyneog came running to give a hand himself, and between them all at last they got the animals to their quarters.

Wolfstan was at the gatehouse, and he and Cyneog greeted one another as old friends.

"I have been looking for you, Wolf. Take these tallies to Brother Severus at the church. He will need them at the end of the day."

The tallies were for the workmen, who could exchange them for goods in payment of their labors. Such matters were often handled by Wolfstan here in Canterbury because he spoke the local tongue. Brother Severus was in charge of the rebuilding at the church of St. Martin, not because he was a builder but because he was a disciplinarian. The church was being mended with love, however, and so he was seldom able to find fault. Therefore he bullied the masons and others whom the King had sent, so that they grumbled and threatened to go home.

Wolf had glanced at Fritha as he took the bag of tallies and started off down the street. He was fairly sure that she would come with him. He heard her say something to her father, then her bare feet padded along the dusty road after him and soon she had caught up. They left the road and crossed the fields between the priory buildings and the church. They found great activity at St. Martin's. The west wall was being repaired and a new supply of brick had just been brought in. Men were bringing the bricks a few at a time on their shoulders. There was a long string of them crossing a nearby meadow and disappearing over a slight mound. Some of the men were laborers from the city, and some were monks, with their gowns kilted up above their knees.

Wolf handed the tallies over to Brother Severus.

"That's a great lot of brick, Brother. Where's it all coming from?"

"It's the when of it, not the where of it, that I care about. We were short of bricks, bricks were found. That is good enough for me."

"I expect it's a hole in the ground," Fritha said. "Often and often bricks come from a hole in the ground."

"You can't dig bricks out of the earth."

"Uthdra found some in a hole and made a new wall."

"That was very clever of him. But you can't," said Wolf obstinately, "dig bricks out of the earth. You mean stone."

"No, I *don't* mean stone."

"Come along, then. I'll show you. Over there—that's where the bricks are coming from."

But when they reached the place, Fritha seemed to be right. There was a gaping hole several feet wide and long. Then they saw what had happened. The workmen had opened up a great heap of earth and stones, and underneath lay the ruins of a house. Out of the ruins they were taking any bricks that were good enough.

As Wolf looked at the place he felt a strange pang. So much of what he looked down on was familiar. It was a house that had been built long ago by the

Romans, and Romans had lived here, and here he saw a score of simple things that made him think of what had been his home. Part of the tiled floor was showing through the dust and rubble and the patterns on the tiles were patterns he had seen a hundred times in Rome. He went into the ruins and began turning the dust over with his toe, tracing the line of leaf and flower and grape. And here, close by what must have been the kitchen quarters, he found an old holed pot like one he had watched Esta stirring over the fire at home. He picked it up and held it, and it was as though he held hundreds of years there in his hand. Here the Romans had come and stayed and built, and they had brought order into the land, and they had turned gradually from the old gods to the new faith. And then they had gone away again. At home their empire had crumbled and there were no longer men enough to leave in this far island while the mother country was threatened.

Wolf knew only a little of this, which had been taught to him when he was in school. But all the lessons he had ever had could not tell him more than this ruined house with its broken ornament and the battered cooking pot covered with earth which he held in his two hands. For as though it were a mirror for his imagination, he seemed to see some solid Roman, coming home quickly from a city council, calling to his wife to gather all they possessed and be ready to leave. . . . And she had dropped the cooking pot and broken it, and it had lain there ever since.

It must have been at that time, Wolf thought, as

though a great bank built against the tide had been broken and torn away. Through the gap left by the withdrawing Romans the barbarian hordes had poured in, bringing dark and bitter days, slaughter and oppression and the return of black paganism.

Now Wolf found himself, with Fritha at his side, wandering through Canterbury with eyes newly opened. Over and over again he saw familiar things— a block of masonry supporting a drinking trough bore a Roman inscription, two delicate pillars carried the front of a barn, a flight of steps leading to a rough stone house had been made from lengths of chipped cornice of a design he had seen often in Rome. And when they came by the city pound, where half a dozen goats and geese waited to be claimed, he saw that this enclosed place had once been a bath. Water still trickled greenly through two ducts, and among the tall weeds lay many broken columns, with bits of their decorated capitals. But the heavy bases had vanished—hauled away, no doubt, as the bricks of the villa were being hauled away to repair the church of St. Martin.

"You are so silent, Wolf. I have news for you, but you won't listen."

"What is it?" he asked quite roughly, for he had been far away and his thoughts seemed hardly to be his own.

"It was not only to sell sheep that my father came here today."

"To sell the sheep and take back grain instead?"

"No, *no!*"

"To buy cloth?"

"Cloth indeed! Do you think my father is rich? He has only the smallest part of the farm. Hardra has the rest. If we want cloth we must weave it ourself."

"Then tell me."

Now he gave her all his attention and wondered that anything so dry and ordinary as dust and stones had distracted him. He might not see her again for months and he was letting the day go by.

"Wolf, my father has come to ask if we may be made Christians."

It was the beginning. That day when Cyneog came to Canterbury and asked if he might speak with Abbot Augustine was the beginning of great things. It was a signal to the people, who though never hostile had yet been reluctant to listen. So many changes had torn the land that they were wary. But Cyneog, who was one of them, offered himself for baptism, and his daughter with him, and from that moment there was keen curiosity. When Augustine preached in the church, in the market place, by the riverside, they began coming to hear him—a few, then many, then a whole flock. They could not understand what he said, and they frowned over Brother Sylvanus' not very eloquent translation. But it was Augustine's manner and his eye and his harsh commanding voice that bound them. They seemed to understand those better than any words. There was little doubt that some of them thought Augustine was himself a god, but gradually they were dissuaded of this, accepting what at first seemed a disappointment.

"Eswige's old father wanted to sacrifice a kid to Father Augustine," Fritha told Wolf, half scandalized and half laughing at such simplicity.

Wolf frowned. But not so much because he was shocked by the tale. He did not relish any talk of Eswige, for she was Uthdra's mother, and Uthdra had still to be reckoned with. Did they understand, Wolf wondered, that when Fritha became a Christian she would no longer be Uthdra's promised wife? Unless, of course, Uthdra became a Christian too. There was great turmoil for Wolf over this. How could he wish Uthdra to remain pagan? Yet how could he honestly welcome him as a Christian?

It was the end of April when Cyneog and Fritha came to the church of St. Martin to be baptized by Augustine. He had chosen the church rather than the riverside, because a great many of the people who had begun to listen were still chary of listening under a roof, and this occasion might draw them in. And so it did. Many who had stood hesitant about the door finally slipped nervously inside. Others moved in with confidence, for they were neighbors who had listened to Cyneog telling them how he had been moved to take this step. They trusted Cyneog, knowing him as an upright honest man whose counsel was worth considering.

Soon the church was at least half full. In the choir the monks followed the lead of their master, Brother

Angelo. Their voices soared in the splendid chants that Pope Gregory had made the rule. The occasion inspired them; their voices had a strong beauty never heard before under that roof.

Wolf was kneeling near one of the pillars. It was a good place—he could see everything. But he was praying hard, too, for Fritha and Cyneog, the first converts, and for all the rest of them, not least himself, and for Ana left so far away in Rome. It was evening and there was a yellow sunlight still at the door of the church and at the arched windows high above their heads. Ana would be sitting down with Ursula and Tullus and the rest to the evening meal. It was already many months since Wolf had seen his sister and he knew she must have grown a good deal. . . .

He pulled himself back guiltily. This was no way to say his prayers on such a great occasion. He looked across to where Fritha and Cyneog were kneeling before Augustine. And as he did so he saw beyond them a woman whose face he knew. Eswige, Hardra's wife, had come to church with the rest.

Now there was silence except for Augustine's voice. By now, Wolf had supposed he knew every note and inflection of that voice. But this evening it was different—so warm with tender welcome, so rich and vibrant with promise that Wolf looked at the face of the man who was speaking and saw it with new eyes. He had found the Abbot severe, almost frightening in the singleness of his purpose and his detachment from the rest. But now Wolf saw a face radiant with a happiness deep and selfless and boundlessly joyful. He heard himself sigh. It was a sigh of comfort and content and brought with it a beginning and an end. It brought a beginning of understanding and an end of "childish things"—which had remained with him though he had long ceased to think of himself as a child. . . .

He heard a little splash and tinkle of water. Augustine had dipped a scallop shell into the great stone jar of water that had been brought to the church and blessed for this purpose. He held the shell and blessed it yet again. Silence held the crowd gathered in the church, and the choir was silent too. Now the water was being poured over the bowed heads of Fritha and Cyneog. The silence still held. The suspense seemed endless. The prayer Augustine was offering over these his first converts was a prayer wordless in its intensity. No one moved. The crowd, the monks, the kneeling figures, the Abbot himself seemed frozen into a timeless pattern which might never be undone.

Then Augustine raised his hand and spoke at last in a voice that was huge and joyous:

"*In nomine Patris* . . ."

Brother Angelo flung up both arms and the monks burst into an immense *Jubilate!* Augustine embraced Cyneog and Fritha, and around them everyone stirred and smiled, still awed, but knowing that this was the moment when joy might replace solemnity. Then they began moving closer until there was a great circle round Augustine, listening far less to Brother Sylvanus, who had hastened to his post as interpreter, than to the

Abbot's voice urging them and advising them and imploring them—longing to embrace them all, longing to see them safely folded and assured of their own place in heaven—as Gregory had promised them in his heart all those years ago when he found Wolfstan and Eobald in the Roman market place.

It was Eswige who broke the circle, making a way for herself to move forward and kneel at Augustine's side. She took his sleeve in both hands, kissing it gently and humbly.

Then a neighbor moved up behind her, then another and another. There was a woman with four children, a man with two sons; there was a grandfather with his grandchildren, a brother with two sisters. . . . Old and young alike they moved steadily closer, pressing in upon Augustine until it seemed as if he might be lost to view beyond the crowd. But even if Augustine had not been a tall man, Wolf thought that at this moment he would still have towered like a giant above all the rest.

Wolf looked round for his father. There was a man standing in the open doorway, but it was not Wolfstan. As Wolf turned his head the man moved quickly away and disappeared into the dusk beyond the door. Wolf was almost sure the man was Hardra.

For some time after the crowd had gone away, Wolf waited to see Fritha. He waited in the church because he was certain she would look for him there. It was now nearly dark and the blackness inside the empty church was pierced only by the small eyes of the altar lights. Wolf grew anxious in case Fritha had gone home after all.

Then he saw her at the door, faintly outlined there in the opening, looking helplessly into the darkness of the church.

"Fritha?"

"Is it you, Wolf?"

He went quickly toward her and took her hand. He spoke at once, before he could have second thoughts.

"Promise me here, before God and His Blessed Mother, that you will never be Uthdra's wife."

Fritha gave him her other hand and they moved together toward the altar, stumbling in the dark on the rough stone floor.

"Kneel down, then," she said. Her voice was very low. She was not like any Fritha he had known till now, but like the Fritha he had thought of sometimes—an older Fritha with a firm mind of her own. "I promise."

"Make it a real vow."

"A promise is stronger," she said. "If we pray over it, that will bind it better than any vow."

They knelt side by side in the silence, and Wolf knew she must be praying better than he was, because he could not find many words.

Then they rose and went outside. Cyneog was looking for his daughter, for it was time to go home. There was a rising moon to see them on their way. Father and daughter looked strong and confident. It was a long journey home, but it held no terrors and their feet might have been winged.

It was much later that Wolfstan came home, hungry for supper, which Wolf had got ready for them both—and full of news.

"We are going on a journey, Wolf."

"Father?"

"I have been with the Abbot and he has given us a mission. We are going to find our old home. We are to speak to the people there and discover what gods they worship. If it seems wise, if the time is ripe, one or two of the brothers will follow and preach. It is a great trust. I am glad of it. I have waited to do some service for the mission. For Pope Gregory. I owe him everything I have."

For a second Wolf did not reply. Then he asked, "When shall we go?"

"Be ready to leave at sunrise."

VIII

The Forest

NEXT MORNING the sky was dull and heavy. The fine spring weather had vanished overnight and Wolf's fine spring spirits had vanished too. He had dreamed of the day when he would see his birthplace. All the way from Rome he had imagined how it would be, and because he was ignorant he had imagined landing on the distant shore and going instantly to the place. But once they were on dry land he had been absorbed by every circumstance great and small as it occurred, and so he had almost forgotten those early dreams. Most of all, Fritha had made the Kentish countryside the place he cared for above any other. Now he must leave it—and without the chance to tell her what was afoot. After the excitements and exaltations of the previous day, this was a sad business.

On the instructions of the Abbot, Brother Adrian had packed food for the travelers.

"If Cyneog and his daughter should be in the city," Wolf said, as he took up the bundle and slung it on his shoulder, "tell them where we are gone."

Brother Adrian gave his dark, rather sardonic smile and said he would do so "without fail."

A pale and watery sun made barely a shadow on the ground as Wolf and his father, with their bundles on their backs, each carrying a stout stick and with a knife at his belt, set out toward the southwest. There was a good firm road that had been laid by the Romans, and although it had not been repaired for untold years and was full of holes and weeds, yet its direction was clearly seen and it was in regular use. In any case, it ran close by the river, crossed it a few miles outside the city, and for many miles more ran within easy reach of the water.

"Will there be a road all the way?" Wolf asked.

"Halfway, so Cyneog said. I cannot remember. Well, I never knew. There was no call to travel then. We had our own roof. We had pasture and growing land, and the forest for wood and game. Life was hard. But it was good. Until the raids. We knew of such things from travelers, but such happenings had been in the north and the northeast. Then all was changed. Each time I went to the fields or to the workings, I knew I might not see my family again."

The workings Wolfstan spoke of were those places where iron was dug and forged. Like everything else, these had fallen on bad times when the Romans left. But the craft continued spasmodically. The skill handed down haphazard from the remotest times seemed too strong to die out altogether. Perhaps it took something from the material it tamed.

"It was the clinker from the furnaces that they used to build the roads," Wolfstan said, remembering slowly. "The Romans, I mean. We knew that much. There was plenty of it. We used it, too. With the stone, it made up a good wall. You could build your house of stone and clinker and roof it with heather thatch. . . ."

In the country they were plodding through now there was no stone. Sometimes there was the ruin of a Roman villa, and sometimes the ruins had been made into a home, or a hut had been built nearby and the villa used to stall cattle. These places seemed full—even in daylight—of gliding, voiceless ghosts. They came, too, upon villages that were clusters of huts round a central farm, and the buildings and the stockade that enclosed them were of wood. Some of the huts were round and thatched with river reeds.

"My grandfather's home was such a one," said Wolfstan.

The people they saw during that first morning were
incurious and ignored the travelers. Living near the
city they were accustomed to the occasional stranger,
but they did not welcome him.

"Should we speak to them?" Wolf asked. "Should
we ask them about their gods?"

"Not here. Too close to the city. It is when we are
farthest that we can do the most."

At noon they sat by the river and ate some of the
bread from their packs. It seemed to Wolf that there
was not very much of it, since they were facing several days' march and had no idea what they would
find at the end of it. But Wolfstan laughed at that.

"Soon we shall be in the forest. There is game for
the catching. We can look after ourselves."

Wolf had never seen this side of his father before.
He had known Wolfstan only as a man attached to
a city way of life. As he spoke of the forest and of
fending for themselves, the years seemed to fall away
from him and he looked like a young and vigorous
hunter.

"We have stayed too long," he said now, getting
briskly to his feet. "Some way ahead the road goes
off to the southwest. That is our way."

"You remember that much, then."

"Cyneog again. He has hunted in the forest borders.
His wife came from a forest village. Pick up your bundle. We should be going."

Now the sky had cleared a little. No one approached them along the highway; none passed from Canterbury on a swift horse. The world was empty of everything but the weedy ruins, the secret villages, and the father and son plodding on to the southwest and the place that had once been home.

That night they camped near the river in a place with a small beach overhung with bushes. In the early evening Wolfstan had killed a hare that crossed their path. They skinned it and made a fire and cooked it. The night was quite warm and very still. The fire was a protection against inquisitive animals but a signal to any possibly inquisitive man. So they were careful with it. Cyneog had said that the forest for a time had been full of robbers and bandits, but now they had been driven out, though there was always the chance of an outlaw on the run.

"It is a pity we have no time to cure this," Wolfstan said, turning the hare's brown coat in his hands.

"We could peg it out on the tree trunk, Father. By the time we return this way the sun may have cured it."

"That is no way to cover your tracks in the forest, Wolf. You must learn better than that. Still"—Wolfstan looked around him in a considering way—"it might be secure enough here. The bushes screen it from the track, but not from the sun."

So the hare's skin was stretched carefully against the trunk of an oak and pinned with sharpened wooden pegs. It was dark by the time they had finished. They

settled down to sleep. Wolf slept at once. Later, opening his eyes, he saw that his father sat on guard by
the fire. Much comforted, Wolf slept again.

Next day they were on the move at dawn. They
covered the fire carefully, ate some of the hard rye
bread and drank from the stream. Before they set
out, they marked the place in their minds, so that
they might return to it. Indeed, they left it regretfully,
knowing that with this second day they moved farther into the unknown. The road would end soon,
so Cyneog had said. Then the forest would swallow
them. Already there were more trees, though broken
by clearings that told them men were about or had
been lately. Now the ruins of the Roman houses, built
by men who had settled at the road's edge for the
sake of communications, grew fewer and at last vanished altogether.

"How far now?" Wolf asked.

"I cannot say, Wolf. I have forgotten too much.
And the tracks I knew may be overgrown by now."

"How will you know the place, Father?"

"By the rise of the land and the stream in the
coombe. By the river that carries the stream along
with it—to the sea, they used to say. Also by the
workings close to the water, where the pond is that
cools the iron as it is beaten with hammers."

That day's going was hard. The road was still there,
but it was more and more sunken into the earth, or
the earth had piled over it. Grass had grown strongly,
and often there were bushes and even trees whose
roots were held among the cracked pavement that

had heaved up into view as the tree grew stronger. What had been won from the forest was almost forest again. And when at last the road vanished, who was to say that it was truly ended? More likely it lay still beneath the undergrowth that had rolled forward over it like a new skin.

In this kind of country it was easy enough to feed on birds and small mammals killed with a stone from a sling. They had bread enough for the time being and there was plenty of water, for they no sooner left one stream than they came to another, or to springs bubbling over stones. And you could see the iron in those stones, where they were streaked with red and a cold blue. All the time they were looking for signs of villages. Often there were clearings from which wood had been lopped and hauled away. Deer abounded, and they were constantly stopped, as the day moved on to dusk, by the sound of their swift movement in the undergrowth. They had always to pause warily and decide whether beast or man thrust through among the shadows.

"If we could catch a deer we should have meat for days," Wolf said.

"We cannot carry it with us."

"We could take what we need and leave the rest."

"That is not good hunting or good husbandry. Kill what you need, no more. There!" he grabbed Wolf's arm as a cock pheasant sailed down into a clearing ahead of them and began picking at the ground. "There is our supper," he whispered.

Wolfstan swung his staff and threw. The heavy

wooden thing thrashed through the air and broke
the bird's back, killing it instantly. Wolf ran forward
and picked up the pheasant. It lay in his hands with
its head lolling, its eyes closed, yet with a tiny beady
slit still showing. The gorgeous feathers, the sweeping tail were things of such beauty as Wolf had never
realized before. The bird was warm in his hands, as
its nest might be if it had only just flown from there.
But the nest soon cooled without the living bird,
and the bird soon cooled with the life fled out of
it. It was food to hand and Wolf was hungry. Yet he
felt a pang of sorrow, of disappointment, almost, that
the bird was dead.

Wolfstan, more practical, at once took the carcass
and began to pluck it. He gave the tail feathers to
Wolf, who stuck them in his belt. The small feathers,
colored and mottled, lay about the clearing.

That night Wolfstan slept first while Wolf kept watch.
There was good shelter there under trees, twenty yards
or so off the track. The little eye of the damped-down
fire seemed to peer at Wolf, who was trying hard not
to nod. It was a night with a full moon in a clear
sky. Intense shadows lay about the camp. There was
a crying of owls about their family affairs, and sometimes a shrill small scream as they pounced and made
off with a mouse or a young rat in their talons. There
was mystery in the night and perhaps an unnamed
danger. Wolf made the sign of the Cross and muttered a prayer under his breath, and then for a time
felt more comfortable.

Then he heard a new sound. It was a rustling and

then a cracking of twigs that had about it something determined and threatening. The darkness and loneliness of the night engulfed Wolf. He imagined great animals with fiery eyes approaching to devour him, or men with knives who would seize him and carry him off, and perhaps kill him on an altar to some pagan god. . . .

Angrily, Wolf shook himself and straightened his shoulders. It was no more than a deer or a fox, or perhaps a wildcat moving with less stealth than cats usually employ.

For a moment or two there was silence. Wolf began to relax. Then he was tense again as a new sound, unmistakable and much closer, came to him from the forest track.

Wolf took his father's arm. He spoke close in Wolfstan's ear as his eyes opened.

"Hush!" breathed Wolf. "There is someone on the track. A man's voice—talking very quietly . . ."

A man would not be talking to himself in the forest in the middle of the night. That meant there were men. Men could spell danger or the comfort of friendliness. Wolfstan rose very cautiously. He had already slipped the knife from his belt. He moved forward slowly, motioning Wolf to follow. The sound of movement along the track continued, but there were no more voices. Perhaps Wolf had imagined that part of it. If so, his father might be angry at being roused for nothing.

Then almost at once the voice came again.

"We must rest," said a man in almost a whisper.

"We have lost their trail now. In the morning we may find it, when it is light again."

Someone gave a deep sigh.

"Are we lost, then? Shall we ever find them? Must we die in the forest?"

Wolf thrust his father aside and rushed forward.

"Fritha! Fritha! *Fritha!*"

IX

Birthplace

F OR A SECOND, in the moonlight under the trees, Fritha did not recognize Wolf. Then suddenly she knew him. But instead of crying out in relief, she covered her face with her hands and burst into tears.

Cyneog put his arms round her in comfort and looked over her bowed head at the others.

"How good to find you, Wolfstan, my friend."

"Why are you here? Were you sent after us? With a message, perhaps? Are we to return?"

At this Fritha cried out in utter misery, "We have lost our home! We have nothing—nothing!"

Wolfstan took Cyneog by the arm.

"We have a camp and a fire and some food. Come, you need to rest."

He led the way through the undergrowth. Cyneog followed, his arm round the still-sobbing Fritha. Wolf, dazed and anxious, followed behind. They came to the camp and Wolfstan made a soft place of last year's leaves and heather for Fritha to lie on. He made Cyneog sit by the fire. He gave them both water and divided what was left of the bread, keeping back some for the morning. Cyneog was hungry but too good a campaigner to eat all he was offered.

"I have some provisions left. I'll take some of your bread to put with the mutton and salt."

Fritha would not eat, but she drank the water thankfully.

"Now tell us," said Wolfstan.

Cyneog groaned and struck his forehead with his fist.

"Fritha has told you. We have no longer a home. Everything is lost. I have not even a weapon save my knife."

"But how, friend? How?"

"All of the farm that was mine is destroyed—the dwelling place, the barn, the byre. The cattle are slain and the geese. There is nothing on my land but a pile of ashes."

Wolf was sitting beside Fritha now and she leaned against his shoulder in an exhausted way.

"We saw the smoke before we reached the place," Cyneog said. "We were nearly home, we were light-hearted and content as never before. God was with us then. It was God who warned us, through Eswige."

"She had gone home before you, then?"

"She was ahead of us by an hour or more. So she was the first to see it. And when she saw she came hurrying back. 'Go!' she said. 'Go, Cyneog, and take Fritha and do not return this way.' "

At first Cyneog had thought she must be mad, for her manner was wild, her eyes staring with fear and dread. "Hardra has burned your home!" she had cried. "Hardra has done it, my husband Hardra. Go at once or he will kill you and give Fritha by force to Uthdra."

"I saw the smoke," said Cyneog, "rising up white in the moonlight. But I turned at once. I could think only of my daughter. We ran into the shelter of some trees and Eswige ran after us, crying out that Hardra would kill me because I am a Christian. Then I urged her to come with us. She would not. 'I love my son,' she kept saying. 'I cannot leave my son.' Then she was gone and I knew all my care must be for Fritha. So we left the road and hid in the ruins of a temple—already there was a sound of men hurrying along the road and I feared it might be Hardra and perhaps others he had roused up against me. So through the night we stayed in hiding and in the morning we went to Canterbury. The brothers gave us food and comforted us, and Brother Adrian told us you had set out some hours before. You were going on a mission to your birthplace, he said."

Cyneog paused. It seemed as though he had come to a part of his story which he could hardly endure to relate. Sitting beside Wolf, Fritha began to cry again, but quietly and sadly, not as she had wept before. At last Cyneog continued.

"I thought we would stay in Canterbury, Wolfstan, but we had been there little more than an hour when a boy came running to the city from our home. He said—he said that Hardra had killed Eswige in his fury, and that he was setting about him like a madman. Then I knew I must take my daughter away from that place. I felt certain you would take the road I had told you of. It seemed to me that if we could find you, then we might make a new home in the place you were going to, for you would speak for us to your people. And since we are now Christians it might be, I thought, that we too could tell them of the true faith. If they chose to kill us, better death that way than at the hand of my brother. Better the chance of life than the certainty of death."

"Thanks be to Almighty God that you are here," said Wolfstan. "There are perils ahead, but we will meet them together. Rest now. Wolf and I will keep guard."

Fritha lay down with a sigh of weariness, but of

relief, too. Wolf pulled off his own rough cloak and laid it over her. He felt as he had done when his mother died—that he had grown years older in as many minutes.

"Go to sleep," he said to her, quite sternly. But he could not help asking, "How did you find our track after the road ended?"

She was already drowsing. "The hare's skin," she mumbled. "The bird's feathers . . ." She was asleep.

When morning came, Wolfstan and Cyneog took counsel together. Although the party was now strengthened there were also twice as many to feed and they did not know how far they were from any village. It was too early in the year to find much help in the hedgerows—there would be no fruit or nuts for many months yet, nor any fungi. When they had had their breakfast that morning there was only a little bread left. It was a fine morning and all about them the forest was thick and quiet save for the birds about their own affairs and the scuttling of small animals among the grass.

Before they left the place where they had made their camp, they gave thanks for a safe night and prayed for help during the coming day. Then they rose and set off again, making due west on Wolfstan's instructions.

Fritha had recovered her spirits after a night's sleep. The disaster of her lost home was behind her and she was content to be here with Wolf and his father. Also she was buoyant with the new faith she had taken upon her. And although in the sunlight she looked once more the tousled girl Wolf had caught spying on the seashore, she had as well an air of gentle contentment that was new.

They walked on through the forest, Wolfstan leading, Cyneog after him, Wolf and Fritha in the rear, walking together. Fritha began to chatter and laugh.

"Be silent, girl!" Cyneog said at last, stopping to frown at her. "We do not know who is about. You make as much noise as a dozen magpies."

Fritha was silent once more, but she looked at Wolf and had difficulty in stifling her laughter. After that, they conversed in dumb show and they were often half breathless as they tried not to laugh.

In about half an hour from noon they saw signs of the movement of men. There was a trodden walk and some timber had been cleared. They followed this warily and came upon a circle of grass and in its midst a huge tree. The tree was an ash and when Wolfstan saw it he flung out his arms as though he would protect the others following behind him. But it was too late, for even Fritha had seen that something dangled in the bare branches from which there rose up lazily three great black birds to circle overhead.

"What is it, Wolf?"

But she knew as well as he, though she had never seen such a thing before. Hereabouts, then, still lingered one of the oldest religions, that had come from the North. This ash tree was Yggdrasill, the tree of the gods, planted by Woden and his brothers, and in the branches hung all that remained of a human sacrifice left there to bleed to death.

"Pass by quickly," Wolfstan commanded, "and pray to God as you go."

They ran by the tree and were away on a long slope leading through many untouched oak trees, trees that made up a sacred grove.

After a time they came to a little river running in a gorge. This would have been a good place to rest and eat, but Wolfstan insisted that they leave the trees far behind.

So it was long after noon before they found another place, and with a river too. They rested and drank and ate what was left of the food. They must catch something for their supper that night.

"Men have been here," Cyneog said suddenly.

Sure enough there were trees lopped and waiting to be dragged away, and the undergrowth was trampled.

Wolfstan looked about him in silence for a long while. He seemed to be measuring the distances, looking to the sun for guidance. He walked a hundred yards or so to prospect from the top of a small hill. Then he came back to the others, who were watching him silently. They saw at once that there was an excitement in his manner, that his eyes shone and he was pale.

"This could be the place," he said in a low voice. "It could be this river that I knew when I was a boy and when I was a young man. Who knows—in another hour I may look upon my home."

"And mine, Father."

"And yours—your birthplace, Wolf." Wolfstan smiled at his son, but sadly. "You have a look of your mother that I never noticed until now."

After that he was silent for a long time, and walked away by himself. He stood with his head bowed. He was thinking of Ea and the cruelly short years they had been together. The others respected his memories and kept to themselves. But the suspense was great. It needed only a brisk march now, if Wolfstan was right, to reach the village and discover the best or worst that was to befall them.

At last Wolfstan came to himself again and returned to the rest.

"I am sure we are in God's hands. He has led us here. With every moment I am more certain. We must go forward. And God's will be done."

"So be it," they agreed, and started on their way.

Now they were all silent. Fritha no longer even gestured a meaning to Wolf, but sometimes took his hand for support as they moved beside the river, treading on an increasingly clear track, where not only trees had been cut but brushwood had been hauled away.

Suddenly the trees thinned away and they were looking down toward a clearing, with dwellings and a stockade. Almost at once there came a sound that made Wolfstan lift up his head. In spite of the uncertainties that seemed to press up to them from all sides, Wolfstan smiled broadly. He caught Cyneog's arm as if urging him to listen.

For the sound was the sound of iron being hammered, and it was many a long year since Wolfstan had heard it. It rang in his ears like a song. It was the sound above all others that he remembered from his youth. This indeed was a homecoming.

The village itself was quiet. At first it seemed deserted. Then as they moved carefully among the dwelling places they came upon a circle of a dozen or more women pounding meal.

For a second the women stared at them blankly. Then one of them began to scream. Instantly there was confusion. The women ran in all directions, all save one old woman who was clearly blind. She still sat with the pounding stone in her hand, her face tilted upward, waiting for what might happen.

Fritha pushed past her father and went to the old woman's side, crouching down close.

"Grandmother, we are friends," she said. She said it again and again, and at last the old woman laid down the stone, which all this time she had held as though it were a weapon, and put her hands on Fritha's.

The women must have run off to find help, for suddenly a dozen or more men came swarming back into the clearing with knives and staves in their hands. A dark, tallish man seemed to be their leader. When he saw Fritha he paused, gesturing the rest to stop where they were behind him. He stood frowning at Fritha, trying to find reason in the presence of a young girl among hostile strangers.

Behind the leader and the other men, the women

crept back and stood in an inquisitive group. Now the children appeared from nowhere and clustered round their mothers, pointing and chattering. The leader took a couple of paces forward and spoke to Wolfstan.

"Who are you? Why do you come?"

"My name is Wolfstan. This is the place where I was born. And my father before me."

"Your father was named—?"

"He was Wolfbert. My wife was Ea, whose father Berthold was killed hunting. I was taken from here, and Ea my wife, and my son who stands here beside me. We were sold into slavery."

He saw them frowning and staring. They seemed to have difficulty in following his words, and a muttering and a questioning broke out among them. He saw that they were slower-witted than he had expected and knew that because he had been taken to far places he had learned without knowing it. He had bettered himself. These were savages still by comparison with himself and Cyneog, though the leader had great presence.

Wolfstan pointed to the old woman. "This might be my grandmother. Save that I know she must have perished on that day the raiders came."

Again the leader frowned and again he asked, "Why do you come?"

"I am a friend. I am a son of this soil that bred you. All here are friends. I am Wolfstan, son of Wolfbert. Here is Cyneog, out of Kent, and Cyneog's daughter. Here is my only son. We ask shelter and food. I lived here and worked the iron. I lived here before I was taken for a slave."

"If so, how are you here now?"

"I was saved by God. By God the Father of all. A great God. God Almighty. Greater than any god you know."

This made them scowl again and mutter to one another. One of them even moved forward threateningly, but he was pulled back by another.

Just then one of the women called out a name. Everyone turned and a newcomer strode in. He came toward the group and instantly the man who had been leader until now fell back and deferred to him. He stared at the travelers, asking quick short questions as he did so and being answered as shortly by the rest.

Wolf, standing beside his father, felt relieved when he saw this man. For one thing, he felt that he knew him. That was absurd, of course, but there was something about him familiar and comforting. He was about twenty, fair, fresh-faced, with keen eyes in an intelligent face. Compared with the rest, he seemed a sage in wisdom. Frowning a little, he approached Wolfstan, then stood looking at him deeply.

"They say you were born here—that you were taken in a raid."

"In a raid that carried off men and women alike, that killed others, that burned the village. . . ."

"What do you say you are called?"

"I am Wolfstan—Wolfstan, son of Wolfbert."

"There was such a disaster as you speak of. I was

a boy then. My mother hid me, but my father and my brothers died or were captured. . . . What was the name of your father's second brother?"

"He was called Wolfig."

"I am his son. I am Sigwolf." He held out his hands. "We are kinsmen."

X

A Good Death

THE MORNING was fine and full of promise as Fritha went to fill the waterpots at the brook. She and the others had been at the village now for many days. Sigwolf had given them a hut to live in, and though it was a tumbledown place, between them they had made it comfortable enough. Each night before they slept, Wolfstan and Cyneog would sit together discussing what should be done next. They were both simple men and now that the task was facing them, they felt very far from confident. Because of their kinship, Sigwolf was ready to listen when Wolfstan spoke of the religion, at once new and old, which had come to the shores of his country. But more was needed than the arguments of a blunt yeoman. Sigwolf was no fool and he seemed to have an answer for everything.

"This god was in our country before," Sigwolf said reasonably. "And our gods rose against him and cast him out."

"He cannot be cast out. He is everywhere, Sigwolf. This I swear to be the truth," Wolfstan said. "He waits only for you to call on Him."

"I don't know about that, kinsman. Cyneog called on him, and what happened? Cyneog's home and all he possessed was burned to a cinder."

"That was because the black devil Satan sits in the heart of Cyneog's brother."

"Why does your powerful god not cast out this devil?" Sigwolf was smiling at Wolfstan, not in mockery, but because he saw that he was finding explanations difficult.

"Any one of the brethren could show you the truth."

"We will speak of it another time."

Fritha was thinking about all this as she watched the pots fill with spring water. She was happy in this place and she had forgotten already the horrors of the burned farm and of Hardra's wickedness. Wolfstan had found here the memory of his youth, of his parents, of the young Ea he had loved and taken for his wife. For Cyneog it was a place of hope where he might settle and make a new life. But for Fritha and for Wolf it was the place where they could enjoy being together day by day, where she was free of the threat of Uthdra. She had not forgotten the night they had knelt in the church of St. Martin, in spite of what had followed so swiftly. In her heart she had done more than promise never to marry Uthdra— she had promised to keep herself for Wolf when he was ready for her.

But as the water brimmed over, Fritha knew, too, that their present situation could only be brief. Wolf-stan must return to tell Abbot Augustine what he had found among his own people, and Wolf would surely go with him. If she and her father remained here in the village, how long might it be before she saw Wolf again?

Two of the young village girls came to the spring as Fritha was turning away. They were sisters, Beada and Crea, and they liked to tease Fritha. Nor was it friendly teasing, but full of sharp malice.

"Do you fill the pots yourself?" asked Crea. "Surely your god could do it for you? You say he is power-ful."

"Ask him to carry the pots home," suggested Beada. "They are very heavy. Ask him, do."

Then they burst into giggles, hiding their faces and leaning against one another for support, they were so shaken by mirth.

Fritha flushed crimson. "It is I who should do things for him."

"My father says no god is greater than Yggdrasill. He is the tree of life. Men pour out their lifeblood in his branches and he gives us good harvests."

Fritha shuddered and turned away. Her heart was beating too fast, it made her breathless. Her happiness had gone. How could she think of living among such people? She felt as her father and Wolfstan felt—sure but helpless.

Beada and Crea followed Fritha along the bank of the little river into which the spring dropped over a hard edge of rock.

"If you fell in the river, Fritha, would your god pull you out?"

"He has saved me before this."

The pots were certainly heavy. It was a relief when the track left the riverbank and turned back toward the village. She could feel the two girls looking after her. She knew they were thinking it might be interesting to push her in the river and see what would happen. As though to prove their malice, a stone hit her hard in the small of the back and she nearly upset the waterpots. The girls burst out laughing. Fritha's eyes filled with tears. She was frightened. When she reached the hut there would be no one there, for Wolfstan and Wolf and Cyneog had all gone hunting with Sigwolf and a score of others. They would not be back before the evening.

The village seemed very quiet when Fritha reached it. Away beyond the first rise in the ground she could hear the sound of the ironworkings. The smell of charcoal was in the air. Ten or twelve small children playing about among the dwellings seemed the only possible company. Then Fritha saw their mothers busy about the usual tasks—cutting and stacking wood, watering the goats, driving the pigs to root among the acorns and beechnuts in the forest. Or scouring cooking pots with sand and setting about the preparation of the evening meal.

Sigwolf's wife, Hedda, had brought in great armfuls of bracken and was spreading it to dry. Later she would use it for bedding. She shouted to her two children as she did so, for they were teasing a neighbor's goat. Then she saw Fritha and called to her.

"Help me with this, will you? There is another lot to be carried. When you need more for yourself, I will help you."

Fritha went gladly to help Hedda. The bracken was young, still curling, which made it soft and springy. This was the best time to cut it for bedding. When it had grown taller and coarser it was good litter for the animals, or bound with the coarser heather that grew in the open parts hereabouts it made thatch for the roofs. When it was youngest of all, barely springing, putting up green shoots straight and tender, then it was good boiled and eaten.

"Are you content here?" Hedda asked Fritha, as she spread and shook out the bracken that smelt sharp and salty, as though it had been dipped in the ocean. "Will you live here? Will your father stay?" She smiled at the girl and said, nodding her head in a pleased way, "My brother Egil would be glad to have you for his wife."

"He is not a Christian," Fritha said, as quickly and firmly as she could.

"He will be a Christian if you wish," replied Hedda easily.

Fritha smiled and then frowned. She did not want to offend Hedda. She knew that Wolfstan had been right when he said, only last night, *The time has come to fetch one of the brethren to speak to them.* Her father had seemed to think it was too soon. But even Fritha was able to see that someone with authority must come soon or great damage would be done.

At noon the women took bread and ale to the men working at the forge or in the fields. Hedda called Fritha and asked her to help. The children came too. They all walked without haste through the forest in the shade, then left the trees and made for the open tilled land, where Hedda's father, and her brother Egil, were working. It was a warm and pleasant day. The chill breeze that tempered the spring weather had gone during the last few days, and summer was here, but a gentle summer.

"Fritha has brought bread for you, Egil," Hedda said.

It was impossible to be haughty with Egil, he was such an amiable lout; but Fritha was reserved enough for him to look a little crestfallen. She wished she had braved Beada and Crea and stayed behind at the village. Suddenly she longed for her own seashore home

and the time, such a little while ago, when she had
been carefree and a child. There had been far less
talk about husbands and wives then, for the matter
of Uthdra had seemed too far in the future to be
worrying. Learning about the new faith and being instructed had set her brain in motion. She had never
so much as seen a book until she and her father went
to be instructed before baptism. Wolf could read and
he could write. This was wonderful to Fritha, who
had never even considered that there were in the
world people who could do such things. In fact, like
Wolf if she had known it, she had grown years in a
few months. The times were such that childhood was
soon over and must be put away forever.

During the afternoon, Fritha helped Hedda clean
her cooking pots, and then wash clothes at the riverside. The water bubbled over flat stones where the
river was no more than a brook, then swept out
broad and deep beyond. A few yards further up the
bank, Beada and Crea were sitting with their bare
feet in the water. They kept looking down toward
Fritha and giggling. And again she had the feeling
that they would not hesitate, if the chance arose, to
give her a shove into deep water.

"Why do they jeer?" she asked Hedda. "I have done
nothing to them."

Hedda was on her knees by the washing stones.
She sat back on her heels and shook her fist at the
girls.

"You idle things! Beada, why do you not help your
mother with the milking? Crea, there'll be a beating

for you when your father comes home if you do not get about your work. Fine wives you'll make when the time comes!"

"Who will be our husbands if *she,* if that witch Fritha, is there to work magic on them?"

At that Hedda rose to her feet. She went swiftly along the bank and before the girls could scramble out of her way she had caught each of them a swinging blow about the ears. Beada burst into wild sobs and ran away. But Crea struck back until Hedda lost her temper and held the girl hard by the wrists, shaking and slapping her. When at last she released her and walked away, Crea replied by spitting on Hedda's shadow. She stooped and picked up a stone and flung it wildly after Hedda before rushing away through the bushes.

"Why does she hate me?" Fritha asked again.

Hedda shrugged. "There was talk of Crea as a wife for Egil. She is jealous and her sister joins in."

Fritha longed to cry out that she would rather die than be Egil's wife, but since Hedda was his sister this did not seem wise or kind. Increasingly she grew impatient for the return of the hunters. She looked restlessly at the sky. The sun was shifting and descending now, but it was still many hours to twilight.

"Carry these," Hedda said, pushing a load of wet cloth into her arms. "We'll hang them over the bushes nearest the hut."

Fritha took the dripping bundle and walked up the track a few paces before Hedda. From here the village was out of sight. There was a small steep climb before the first hut was reached. But as she started up the little path worn deeply by the feet of women coming daily to the water, Fritha heard voices. She heard a woman cry out as though in horror. Then came a babble of confused cries.

For a second Fritha stood frozen.

Hedda called out, "What is it?"

"Something has happened. A disaster."

As she spoke, she began to leap up the track toward the village with Hedda behind her stumbling and panting.

"The children!" Hedda cried. "The children!"

Terrible, wild conjectures filled their imagination—that raiders had swooped down and would carry them off—that the village was burning—that a pack of wild beasts had come out of the forest to devour everything in sight. . . .

They reached the clearing and saw at once that none of these things had happened. The hunters had returned. Their kill was slung down in a heap, the huge body of a stag arched over a mound of hares and rabbits and birds.

But the men were clustered round a figure prostrate on the ground.

"Someone killed in the hunt!" cried Hedda. "Not Sigwolf! Not Sigwolf!"

She rushed past Fritha, who stood helplessly, deafened by the beating of her heart, unable to look.

At Hedda's approach the crowd parted a little to let her through. Was it Sigwolf? No, for there he was on his knees beside the man on the ground. Wolf-

stan, then? Wolf? Or only some stranger? Still Fritha
dared not look. She shut her eyes and stood rigid,
waiting for a voice.

"Fritha!" someone said. "Come quickly!"

It was Hedda, who had returned and took her by
the hand and led her forward.

"Cyneog. . . ." Hedda said.

Whatever had happened, her father had always been
there. When her mother died, when the sea came in
one spring and swamped their home, when the farm
was burned and Hardra threatened death, Cyneog had
remained, firm and steady.

Wolf was at Fritha's side. "It was a huge boar, tusked
like a bull. The greatest kill of the day, and it was to
be mine. All the men agreed. They stood back. But I
slipped, Fritha. I slipped like a fool. Cyneog sprang
forward, and it was he, it was he . . ."

"Is he dead, Wolf?"

"He cannot live."

Fritha's heart steadied and she grew calm. She
moved forward and they made a way for her. Cyneog
was lying with his head on a heap of bracken and
someone had covered him with a cloak. His eyes were
open. There was blood trickling from his mouth.

"The tusk gored him," Sigwolf said in a low voice.
"There was swampy ground. He slipped, as Wolf had
done. He fell and the beast trampled and gored him.
His ribs are broken. His lungs are pierced. It is a wonder we got him here alive."

Accustomed to death and violence, they were hushed
by it none the less. A man dying in battle might ex-

pect a glorious afterlife with the gods, but a man dying by accident—how would it be for him? And they stared uneasily at Wolfstan, who was kneeling by Cyneog and praying aloud, praying frantically for help, for comfort and strength.

"No god is strong enough to save him," Sigwolf said quietly. "He must go."

"Oh, God Almighty," prayed Wolfstan, over and over, "take his soul in mercy. God, Our Father in Heaven, call Cyneog home who saved my son. . . ."

Fritha put her head down close beside her father's and without moving any part of him but his eyes he seemed to come from very far away to greet her. His lips did not move, but his eyes smiled. She slid her hand into his and held it. Then his gaze moved heavily and slowly from Fritha's face to another close by her. She knew he was looking for Wolf. She reached for Wolf's hand and laid it with her own beneath Cyneog's. Their two hands felt his heart beating, now faintly, now leaping like a fish against a net, desperate to escape.

Now Wolfstan was silent, his face buried in his hands. He was utterly stricken by his own pitiful inadequacy. He knew too little, he who had been saved and taught and brought back to his homeland to speak of his beliefs. He knew nothing now save that Cyneog must die and there was none near to speak over him those last prayers which might comfort his departing spirit.

When Wolfstan ceased praying, the silence was intensified among the rest. There was no sound but Cyneog's difficult breathing. His eyes had closed now, but his hand laid over Fritha's and Wolf's still seemed to have some strength in it.

Quite suddenly he moved. He gave a harsh cry and raised his head. His hand grasped at the two beneath it. He tried to speak, and then cried in a loud clear voice that made many of them there cower in something like terror: "Into thy hands, O Lord . . . Into thy hands . . . Into thy hands . . ."

He could not manage any more, or perhaps he had forgotten, for he was a very simple man and what he had learned had been committed to a memory untrained. He looked for an instant puzzled, worried. Then his eyes closed slowly and gently and he sank back with a sigh almost comfortable. His grasp slackened and broke altogether as his fingers opened.

"Father," Fritha said.

He did not open his eyes again, but he smiled. His smile began very gently, then widened until his face in the moment of its dying became joyful and almost gay.

They all moved forward to see him. For though he was gone from them now, the sign of his great contentment remained upon his dead face, and he looked like a young and carefree man again, pleased with some task ably performed.

"It was a good death," someone said.

They all began to murmur and to nod their agreement. A good death it had been, full of courage and grace, almost as good as a death in battle. Yet not so good, for their warriors could be sure to return if need be in another body to fight again.

"He will not return."

"Nor would he need to," said Wolfstan. "Where he has gone, the battle is over. He shall live forever in peace and honor and joy."

No one answered this for a long time. They stood looking at the dead man's smiling face. For the first time since Wolfstan had returned among them, they seemed to be considering.

Then Sigwolf took Wolfstan's arm and raised him to his feet. With his hand on Wolfstan's shoulder he said gravely, "Fetch your priests here, then, kinsman. We will shelter them and protect them, if they will teach us to die as well as Cyneog died. This is my solemn oath—to shelter, to protect, to learn. . . ."

And he looked round him at the men there, and one by one they nodded in solemn agreement.

"Aye. To shelter, to protect, to learn. . . . It needs a good god to give a man a good death."

At the next sunrise, Wolfstan turned his back on the village and headed once more for Canterbury. Hedda had tried to keep Fritha, and Egil had offered to take her for his wife. But Fritha knew Wolfstan would not consent and she was never afraid. Her own father had bound her to Wolf with his dying hand. She said goodbye to Hedda sadly, for all that, for it was the first time any woman had treated her as Hedda had done, as more than a child. The brief friendship had given Fritha new confidence.

The return journey was quiet. Their loss was very heavy upon them, and Fritha wept often. But warring with their sorrow and their loss was the knowledge that Cyneog's death had not been wasted. It was he who had proved the best missionary of them all.

Because of the fine weather and the urgency of the message they carried, they made good time on the return. On a fair soft morning they came within sight of the city. They looked down from rising ground and suddenly saw that great numbers of people were on the roads. From all directions they were converging on Canterbury, purposefully making good speed on the rough ways.

"Why are they coming in from the countryside? Have they been driven by raiders?"

But somehow the urgency about the hurrying crowds, even seen at such a distance, did not seem like the urgency of fear.

"Ask this fellow," Wolfstan said, waiting until a man overtook them who was followed by a small crowd of his own—wife, children, parents.

"It is the King!" the man cried. "Have you not heard? The King sent for the Abbot. Hour after hour they talked together. The King seeks baptism. King Ethelbert is to be made Christian."

"Is it certain?"

"It is proclaimed in all the country. The King will be baptized. So we are going to see this done. And to learn the same wisdom, if we are able. They say it is the same for King and peasant alike. This is indeed wonderful. All may serve this god and do him honor and reach salvation. Is this what you have heard?"

"This," said Wolfstan in a great joyful voice, "is truth itself."

XI

The King's Day

AS THE THREE travelers continued toward the city
they became part of the moving crowd. It was
hard to believe that so many people lived in this part
of the country. And soon from their talk it appeared
that many came from farther north. News of the King's
conversion had spread from mouth to mouth as trading

up and down the countryside and around the coast
took its usual course. It would take many weeks and
months, no doubt, for the news to reach the most
distant corners of the kingdom, but it had spread already beyond the ancient Roman city of London, prob-
ably as the result of a chance remark of the King's
overheard by a servant and passed by him to his
friends. Indeed it might almost be supposed that the
news of the King's decision had been spreading even
before he himself had finally made up his mind. Because of Queen Bertha's faith the fact that the King
might come to worship her god had long been spoken of. The ground was therefore rich and fertile
when the seed of gossip at last dropped into it.

The day was fine. It was the second of June. The
trees were in splendid leaf, their green fresh and tender. By the wayside, the hawthorn flowers still lingered
and dog roses were bursting into bloom. There was
meadowsweet and buttercup and campion, and under
the trees in stretches of woodland the last bluebells
and a few late primroses.

Wolfstan looked around him at the crowd in an
awed fashion. "I cannot count the numbers. We might
be in Rome when the people go to the Colosseum
on a holiday."

Mostly indeed the people seemed in a joyful holiday mood, but here and there could be seen solemn
groups who kept always together. These, it was certain, had come to bewail the King's desertion of the
old gods.

"Have they come from my old home?" Fritha won-

THE KING'S DAY   153

dered. "What if my Uncle Hardra should come—and Uthdra too?"

"We shall protect you," Wolf said.

But he looked at his father and frowned a little. Fritha's situation was a difficult one. She had no home to go to now that her father was dead. It was unthinkable that she should return to the village where Hardra and Uthdra waited. It was hard to see what was to become of her. She and Wolf were too young to marry and yet there was no woman to care for her if she came to live with him and his father. It was clear that some solution of the problem must be found quickly. Meantime, the events of this day claimed them.

By the time Wolfstan, with Wolf and Fritha, came near the door of St. Martin's church, a great procession was already on its way across the meadows to the river. It was there that the King's baptism was to take place, so that as many as possible might see it.

First came every monk of the community, carrying great banners and swinging censers from which blue clouds of sweet burning incense rose on the summer air. As they went, the monks sang together, chanting psalms according to the rules laid down by Pope Gregory himself. Then came the senior members of the community and the cross, borne today by the youngest monk, Brother Simplissimus. Behind the crossbearer walked Abbot Augustine, taller than any there. His head was lifted and the sun shone on his strong face, in which pride and humility seemed to struggle together. Proudly he led the King toward the King of Heaven, and humbly he made the offering of his convert.

Behind the Abbot the King walked alone. He wore a simple, belted tunic to his knees, and his head was bare. He held his hands lightly clasped before him and frowned as he went, for this was for him a moment of great solemnity. He knew, as Augustine knew, that hordes would follow him; not all from a true intention, but many because he was their King and what he thought must necessarily seem right to them. And out of this might come great good—or evil. After the King came Queen Bertha, her chaplain, Bishop Liuthard, her ladies and her eldest son. Behind them again, nobles and leaders of the court.

It was a slow business, moving in that ever increasing crowd to the river. Wolf held Fritha's hand, afraid he might lose her in the crush. In spite of the joyful solemnity of the occasion, he was looking this way and that the whole time, afraid he might suddenly see Hardra's revengeful face, or Uthdra's, keen with malice. Wolfstan was close on their heels, so Fritha was by no means unprotected. None the less, both Wolf and his father were aware that in a crowd such as this one it would be easy to snatch her away and escape. She should never have returned to Canterbury while Hardra lived, but what else could they have done but bring her with them?

At last they reached the meadow. The crowd spread out along the riverbank. Some who wished for a better view and could not take time or trouble to walk back to the ford, slid into the water and swam across. Soon

THE KING'S DAY   155

there were as many on one bank as on the other, all
gazing toward the King, who had now moved to the
ground chosen and kept clear for the ceremony.

The riverbank sloped away here, and there was a
little beach. The monks, still chanting, formed a semi-
circle, enclosing the spot and making of it a place of
prayer and worship. The sunlight, so clear in the bril-
liant sky, laid a glossy splendor on the scene. Though
the bulk of the people there were poor, with rough
clothes and dirty faces, on this day they seemed twice
themselves. Gradually the faces of those who had come
to grumble took on a fresh expression. Most of them
had never seen the King before, many others had
never even seen one of his nobles; and their dress
alone, the red of cloaks and tunics, the silver and
copper and gold ornaments that glinted in the sun,
drew cries and sighs of admiration.

Soon round the outskirts of the crowd, among those
too far away to take any proper part in the ceremony,
beggars began to move with whining cries, imploring
food and money. They had come from the crumbling
parts of this city and the nearby port, where they
lived like rats in a sewer and were barely seen by
daylight. They were ragged and filthy, covered with
sores and often short of an arm or leg, an eye or
ear.

"What do they think?" Wolfstan muttered. "That
this is a fair or a market? Be off!" he cried to one
who came near. "Or else listen and watch, and pray
that what eyes you have may be opened."

It was foolish and fruitless advice and harsh, too,

for these were the remnants of humanity whose avarice was the fruit of their bitter poverty. And what could they know of prayer, who had never been taught?

Now the excitement was mounting. Fritha and Wolf forgot about Hardra and began to move away from Wolfstan, making for the place where the crowd was densest, hoping to take a nearer part in the ceremony. They eased and slid between men and women craning to see over the heads of their neighbors. In this way they contrived to come where they could not only hear the singing clearly, but where Wolf could also recognize those he knew best among the monks. Then he saw that they had come, without realizing it, close where the Queen was kneeling on a little cushion set for her by one of her ladies. She wore a purple cloak and a white veil, and over the veil the golden circlet that was her royal crown.

"She looks so pale," Fritha whispered. "Her hands are like lilies. Is it because she is sick, or just because she is a lady?"

"How should I know?"

"They say she need do nothing all day but say her prayers and sing to her children. Could that be true?"

"Look. It will happen soon. Watch!"

Suddenly the singing ended. The crowd gave a whispering murmur and then was silent. The voice of Augustine was heard, then, not only by those close at hand, but by hundreds. He raised his hand to bless and make holy the water that would baptize the King, crying as he did so, "*Exorciso te, creatur aquae, in nomine Dei Patris omnipotentis. . . .*"

Fritha's head was bent, and her two hands covered her face. Glancing at her, Wolf remembered that other baptism, when she and her father had knelt before Augustine in the dark church of St. Martin. He saw how that first ceremony had been a preparation for this one, the first link in a chain that now held the King himself, binding him to all those behind and ahead whose faith and purpose were the same as his.

The silence of the crowd became a humming silence of anticipation as the Abbot held out his hand to the King and they went down together to the water.

At once the King dropped on his knees and the water by the little beach flowed about him, gently yet steadily. Augustine, his crossbearer at his shoulder, stooped, scooped up the water of the river he had blessed into his two hands and praying poured it over the King's bowed head. Then the Abbot knelt, and the singing broke out above them in a tumult of praise. The King bowed his head until his brow was against the waters of the river. Then Augustine rose. He raised up the King and embraced him. As the King stepped back to the bank, Augustine lifted his hand and made a great sweeping sign of the Cross that embraced the whole mighty crowd gathered in the meadows.

A sharp whisper ran among the crowd. A few held up their arms to shield their eyes, as though not daring to let this blessing come upon them. Others furtively made the sign against evil. Most, however, seeing their King come from this ordeal not only whole but with a smile of great contentment and joy upon his face, accepted what was offered, even though they could not understand. Later they would say among themselves *I saw what he did. I knew why he did it.* Or *I was the better for it.* And *This god speaks with a good voice.* For they knew only that Augustine was the god's priest and imagined that his great voice was the voice of the god speaking through his servant.

Gradually the procession re-formed. The singing began again. But now it was like the joyous shout of angels, huge in triumph, rich in contentment. Whereas on approaching this place they had moved with solemn deliberation, now they seemed to surge forward, as though the singing carried them.

The people started running, first ahead of the procession, then after it, then hurrying at its side. The King and the Abbot walked together now, water still dripping from their clothes, which were wet to the thigh from the river. The monks surrounded them, but every now and again they were caught up in the tumult of the crowd. There might be a darting figure stretching out a hand to touch the King or Augustine, then falling back quickly, almost shyly, as though overcome by the daring of it. And all the time the slow talk of the people was like a background to the singing, as they constantly repeated the names of Ethelbert the King and Augustine the Abbot, over and over and on and on, like a litany or an incantation of their own, across the meadow to the wide pathway leading through the city to the church of St. Martin. There at a solemn Mass of thanksgiving, the King would make his communion.

Wolf and Fritha were still standing near the Queen. She had remained all this time with her face buried in her hands and none had felt able to interrupt her prayers. It had been said she had lacked zeal or the King would have embraced Christianity years ago. But he was a proud man, that could be seen at a glance, and she could not have been so very neglectful or he would not have offered himself so soon to Augustine.

It was only a few months since that day the mission had landed on the Isle of Thanet, utterly uncertain of what might be in store. It was through the Queen that they had been welcomed, and because of her they faced now great opportunities and the firm hope of progress. Looking at the Queen's bowed head, both Wolf and Fritha felt a great warmth in their hearts.

Now the Queen was rising and Bishop Liuthard had stepped near to hold out his hand and help her to her feet. They began to move away after the rest, the ladies clustering around. One furtively brushed the grass from her skirt and frowned a little at a green stain. A number of men at arms appeared as from nowhere, and the Queen's procession was soon moving away over the meadow and out of sight like all the rest.

The meadow was empty of all save Wolf and Fritha, and the little cushion the Queen had knelt on to save her from the grass.

Wolf stooped and picked up the cushion. As he did so he heard his father shouting from the roadway.

"I have been looking for you. I have news."

They ran across to him at once, full of their own excitement.

"We were close by the Queen."

"How beautiful she is!"

"A boy from your home came searching for me, Fritha," Wolfstan said. "There is nothing to fear now from Hardra. For the murder of Eswige he was to die, but Uthdra freed him in the night and they both took their boat and sailed away. By now they are in a new country, or even drowned, if they have their deserts."

This abrupt return to everyday matters was somehow hard to accept. The events of the morning had transported them into some other world. Now they found that problems remained. If Hardra was gone and the danger with him, what then?

"Wolf and I will take you home, Fritha. You have others there who will care for you. This is so, is it not?"

"There is my mother's sister. . . ."

"Then we will go to her."

Fritha's eyes filled with tears. She looked at Wolf. He was frowning, almost scowling at his father.

"She is not a Christian," he said at last.

"Today will mean many, many conversions. Fritha shall be a missionary in her own village."

"She should have some Christian woman to care for her," Wolf insisted.

Wolfstan became exasperated. "How can this be?"

"It must be, Father. Cyneog gave Fritha to me as he died. And I say that she must be cared for by a Christian woman."

"But we know no Christian woman, boy!"

"We know one," said Wolf. "The Queen." He tucked the embroidered cushion under his arm and held out his hand to Fritha. "We must wait by the church door until she comes. She will give us a boon in return for this cushion. This is a day for queens to grant boons. She will listen, Fritha. She will care for you."

It was late evening when Wolf made his way to the monastery kitchen and found Brother Adrian clearing up after a hard long day.

"Rejoicing will always lead to feasting," he complained, "and that is hard on all cooks." He looked from under his black eyebrows at Wolf. "Where have you been? You reached home this morning, for I saw your father and heard what he had to tell. Could you not have come to work?"

"I saw the King baptized, Brother."

"So did we all, praise God for it."

"And then I spoke with the Queen."

"Indeed," said Brother Adrian. "Truth is a great virtue."

"I am speaking the truth, Brother. The little kneeling cushion was left in the meadow. I took it to her."

"You are going up in the world. Better carry cushions for queens than meal and maize for Brother Cook."

"I will work now, Brother," Wolf said, grinning. "My father is with the Abbot. There is much to tell him. I will scrub the floor for you."

The brick floor of the kitchen was scrubbed every

day at the very least, for Brother Adrian was fussy
about beetles and mice. He sat himself down on a
bench as Wolf fetched a pail of water, and flexed his
tired feet, which had been chafed by his sandals; he
had spent such a long time standing and running
from oven to table. He began to ask questions about
the journey past while Wolf started scrubbing, and
he groaned when he heard of Cyneog's death.

"God rest his soul as he deserves—he may have
brought many into the fold by the manner of his dying. And what of his daughter, now?"

Wolf did not look up when he answered.

"The Queen has promised to care for her."

"She is a lady the Mother of God herself has
blessed," Brother Adrian decided. "So the girl will
be one of her household."

Wolf nodded. He felt himself redden as he scrubbed.
He had many things to remember of that day. Of
course he must remember that it was the King's day.
But Wolf felt a long way from the King, in spite of
everything. He was the Queen's man, rather. What he
remembered most then was the Queen's surprised
soft smile, when he had begged a way to her, then
her interest, then the way she had taken both of Fritha's
hands and held them and told her to be comforted,
for her father's soul was surely safe in heaven. . . .
Then the Queen had said, looking about her at her
ladies and her chaplain and the rest: "I am to found
a convent, a sisterhood. Who knows, this young maid
may one day be its Abbess."

It was this in particular that Wolf, as he scrubbed

the floor vigorously, blushed to recall. For he had seen that the Queen was speaking not altogether in jest. He had been bound to speak out.

"No, lady," he had said firmly, as though he were the Abbot himself and able to contradict even a queen. "No, lady, for she is my betrothed. Her father clasped our hands together as he died, and we have sworn an oath to be husband and wife one day. In the church of St. Martin, on the day of Fritha's baptism, this was the promise we made."

The Queen had looked at Fritha and asked if this was so, and Fritha had replied *Yes* in a faint but firm voice. This time as she turned back to Wolf, the Queen was really smiling. "Then this is my promise. I shall keep her in safety for you. But it must be for seven years," she said.

As he remembered this, an immense happiness and contentment touched Wolf. God knew it was a long time to wait, but it was just, and they would endure it. . . .

"Take care!" cried Brother Adrian.

It was too late. The bucket was knocked over and the water was spreading all over the floor. Not that it mattered. It would have needed a deluge to disturb Wolf just then.

An hour later the kitchen was clean and tidy. As Wolf threw out the last pail of water, the bell rang for the last office of the day. He left the kitchen as the monks began making their way to the chapel. The chapel was in the crypt of the building, which increasingly gained dignity as the brothers worked

on its restoration. Wolf flattened himself against the
wall to allow them all to pass. Their sandals flapped
on the stone floor; there was a swish of long robes.
They walked with their hands in their sleeves and
their eyes downcast.

They went by silently, contained within themselves.
The day had been a great day—they were weary as
well as exalted. Each man seemed to carry with him
a new happiness and a new confidence. They had set
out a year ago from their own sun-warmed country
and come to this chilly island. They had done it for
the love of God and they had often faltered, but today they had seen the beginning of their reward. The
excitements were over, the King returned to his own
dwelling, the crowds dispersed. Now they were left,
this small community, to their own humble prayers.
It was only a beginning—they all knew that. The
hard work that lay ahead, the hazards of thrusting
on into a country still bound in its majority to paganism, the tussle with forces so long familiar that
they were in the very roots of the people—these tri-
als they accepted calmly, for they were the just dues
of their calling.

At the end of the double file of monks, in the place
of a shepherd driving forward a willing flock, Augustine walked with tireless dignity. Unlike the others, he
was looking straight ahead of him. There was a faint,
unfamiliar smile on his face that proclaimed his contentment with this first great step. The next step was
already before him, and the King himself had that day

given the sign that it must be taken soon and taken boldly.

"You have set my feet this day on the steps to Heaven," King Ethelbert had said. "Now I will set yours on the steps of a throne. The Pope already urges you to seek consecration as a bishop. I have another prayer, and one I know will be granted. We shall speak of you soon, Father Abbot, as the first Archbishop of Canterbury."

XII

The Foundations of the Future

THE KING was in Canterbury. It was the seventh
spring from the day of the Queen's promise, for
even seven years will pass. Wolf was sent for.

"I have been reminded of what I owe," the King
told him. "Here is the title to the land we have prom-

ised you may call your own. Take it, boy, and may you prosper."

"May the King prosper!" cried Wolf. He went on one knee and took the roll. "May God bless and keep your lordship always."

"Amen to that. Now be off with you. And since every man must needs get to his spring planting, the Queen has released you from the last months of the vow. You may claim the girl tomorrow."

Wolf stammered something, but the King had already turned to other matters, and he knew himself dismissed.

The land the King had given Wolf and Fritha was outside the city and along the river, not too far from the great new monastery and church that were being built, which would be dedicated to St. Peter and St. Paul. For about the monastery and the monastery lands, Wolf's work would always lie. Nowadays, though Wolfstan gave the orders, Wolf saw them carried out. Increasingly there was church property to be administered—farms and villages, granaries and herds, dovecots and stewponds, and the sea fishery which provided winter fare for the monks and the poor they fed in great numbers. And if they had not thrust on as far westward into the forest as had once seemed likely, they knew the time would come. If they had learned nothing else in these years, Augustine's men had learned patience.

They had been busy, too, all this time. When the Pope elevated Abbot Augustine to become the first Archbishop of Canterbury, he sent a blessing: "*All the*

Bishops in Britain we commit to your care." And a
year later the Holy Father sent to England many wise
and learned brethren to assist in the great work of
converting the country. Mellitus came, and Paulinus,
with Laurentius and Justus and Rufianus. What had
been a small, struggling mission based on a modest
community, became now a church established and
growing hourly. In the years that followed the conversion of King Ethelbert, Augustine's work prospered.
Hundreds were baptized. The old gods were thrown
down. Young men came to devote themselves to the
religious life—already some of these were nearing their
final vows.

Much had been accomplished, but the Archbishop
was no longer a young man, and he had been in poor
health for many months.

As Wolf left the King's apartment, his head full of
thoughts of the future, the gatehouse porter, Brother
Hugh, called to him.

"I have been looking for you. There has been a
fellow asking to speak to you. I sent him to your
house to wait."

"Who was it, Brother? What was his business?"

"He did not say. I never saw him before."

Wolf swallowed his irritation. He wanted only to
go straight in search of Fritha, and now this matter
must be dealt with.

"Very well. I will go and speak to him. He is prob-
ably from the coast—we are to build more fishing
boats."

THE FOUNDATIONS OF THE FUTURE   169

Outside his own door, Wolf saw a young man standing. He was tall, heavily built, with black hair—at
once familiar and unknown. As Wolf approached, the
stranger turned.

"Wolf?"

"Yes?"

Then his hands clenched into fists of rage and
fear.

The man was Uthdra.

"Well?" said Wolf at last. "You are here. And your
father?"

"Long dead."

"Why have you come back?"

"Where is Fritha?"

"Where you cannot touch her."

Uthdra cried out, "Not dead?"

"Dead to you. She is my promised wife. Her father,
Cyneog, gave her to me with his dying breath. The
Archbishop himself consents and will marry us. And
the King has given us land. And the Queen has cared
for Fritha, who is mine and no other man's."

Uthdra laughed. Wolf looked at him sharply and
curiously. The laughter was not as he would have expected, taunting and harsh. It was quite gentle, almost teasing. Uthdra had changed. His face was not
the black-browed loutish face that Wolf remembered.
It was firm, open, curiously gentle.

"Uthdra, what do you want of me?"

"I want your hand in friendship, Wolf. Do not
think of me as my father's son. That night we sailed
away a storm upset our boat. Hardra was killed and

I was picked senseless from the waves by fishermen. I was half dead and they left me with the monks nearby. There I have been these many years—"

He paused and Wolf waited, frowning now. If Uthdra was a Christian, might his earlier betrothal to Fritha hold firm in the eyes of the law?

"Wolf, I am your friend and ask only that you should be mine. From tomorrow, my life is to change."

"From tomorrow?"

"Tomorrow I enter the Order of St. Benedict here in Canterbury. Meet me twenty-four hours from now and you will meet a novice."

A great gush of relief made Wolf grab Uthdra by both hands. Never had he felt such brotherly warmth toward any man as he felt then. It was a very human, a very secular warmth, he realized a little guiltily, but he would surely be forgiven for feeling happier that Uthdra was relinquishing Fritha, than that he was relinquishing his life in the world for one of dedication to God.

At last Wolf was free to hurry to the Queen's bower, where she and her ladies had their rooms. As he went he was filled with nervousness. Tomorrow he would fetch Fritha and she would never return to the Queen's household. But suppose she had had some change of heart which she had not yet admitted? What if the seven long years had turned the thoughts of his promised bride toward a different future? The Queen had by now founded her sisterhood, and the convent was filling with women eager for the religious life. What if, on this very day of all days in time, another new novice should take a vow very different from the one Wolf had in mind for her?

He wiped the palms of his hands against his sides. He fingered the parchment deed that meant his future was assured. But he would never make his house for any other woman, and if he should be thwarted of his choice now he would live and die alone.

He looked about him for the porter or a guard, but the courtyard was deserted. Then he heard singing. It came from the Queen's little chapel that she had lately built close to her own apartments. Wolf moved toward the chapel apprehensively. The sound of women's voices singing in unison played on his imagination. Until a few seconds ago it had not occurred to him that he might still lose what he had desired so long, but now suddenly it seemed far more likely that he would lose than gain. When the Queen laid down the hard condition of a seven-year period of waiting, he thought in his panic, she must have known she was likely to prevail.

He stood by the chapel door and was afraid to go inside. Now he could hear that there must be many of the sisterhood celebrating together. What if they were already receiving the novice—cutting off her hair, laying the long fair locks on a silver platter to be set aside as an offering upon the altar? If it was so, it would be of her own choice, he knew that, for she was not one to be prevailed upon or persuaded against her will. If after all she had rejected him, without warning, if he was to be alone . . .

He pulled open the door and slid into the dark chapel. The sun had been bright outside and at first he could not see even the starry pattern of the lighted candles, or the glow of the great tapestry he knew lay stretched across the altar. He could feel without seeing that the chapel was full. Then gradually, as though some small particular dawn were breaking, the place took shape before him. He saw what he had expected to see—the Queen, her ladies and waiting women, the black-clad nuns, the officiating priest, the kneeling girl, the hair at that very moment being sheared.

Wolf started forward as though he must shout in protest, whether it was sacrilege or not. But a hand slid over his mouth. He was pulled backward from the aisle and almost fell. He snatched at the hands muffling him. They were small and soft. A well-known voice spoke in his ear:

"It is Ethswitha, the Queen's second daughter, taking her first vows."

Faint with relief, he fell on his knees and Fritha knelt beside him, now holding both his hands and whispering in reassurance.

"What did you think?"

"That it was you."

"I? I made my first promises long ago—have you forgotten? It was in the dark church of St. Martin on the day I was baptized. Seven years of novitiate, Wolf. Now there is only the final vow to take."

They stayed side by side in the shadows at the back of the chapel as the ceremony proceeded to its end. Then the nuns took their new sister in their midst and singing joyously they moved in procession through the chapel, carrying her away.

"Come with me," Wolf whispered. "We are released from the last months. We may be wed tomorrow. The King has given me the deed and the land is mine. Come with me and see the place."

Fritha looked over her shoulder nervously.

"Now? If I come with you alone, someone may see us."

This was the new Fritha speaking, the girl who after these years among gentle people herself spoke softly and moved smoothly. Yet somewhere hidden in all this was still a sturdy country girl who would work beside him in the fields, if need be, and there was the child he had seized by the wrists and taken prisoner, years ago on the seashore. That was the Fritha who had crept out often enough during the past years, wearing the rough clothes she had been accustomed to until her father died, passing easily for anyone's servant girl, not one who waited on the Queen.

"Muffle your face, Fritha, and come. The place is not wholly mine till we have been to it together."

"Wait in the street, then."

Outside, the sun was still shining. He waited a long while in the street. Now it was nearly noon. There were few people about. Either they were pausing for the midday office, in which lay folk were encouraged to join, or they were seeking shade for a few minutes' rest from labor, or they were calling for food.

Presently she came through the gateway and walked toward Wolf. Fritha had an old hood pulled low on her forehead and she had smeared her face with dust. Wolf laughed and caught her hand and rushed her away from prying eyes.

It did not take them long to reach the place.

"This is it," Wolf said. "First we must live in the hut. It was here waiting for us. My father and I have mended the roof and made it sound. Later we will build ourselves a home. As I grow older I shall become more skilled, and as the church lands increase, so too, God willing, will my work. And its reward. Look, Fritha, here is where our children will be born and grow. Here is where you and I may die."

She said nothing. She stood looking about her. She looked at the river and at the fertile meadow, at the building on the far bank, rising up nobly against the sky. She walked about the plot where the hut stood that would shelter them for a time. It was built into an angle of stone, so that two walls were solid and two of timber. She looked at this and frowned.

"There were others here before us, then. Look, Wolf, this stone is a wall."

She went down on her knees and began plucking at the grass round the base of the wall. A carpet of grass and roots and earth peeled back as she tugged it, revealing flat stone beneath—a floor, colored tiles decorated with the familiar pattern of vine leaf and running animals.

Wolf stood beside the kneeling girl and stared down at the floor. His imagination seethed with pictures—

Rome, his other home, the houses of the rich and powerful where he had had no place, and their ruined counterparts he had so often seen in the broken places of Canterbury. He thought of his sister Ana, and the news of her that had come with the last letters sent to the Archbishop from Rome—how she was married a year ago, not to Tullus but to his younger brother, and already had a son of her own. And standing here in England, with a girl of the country, upon stones laid by Roman hands, it was as though the different threads of his life were suddenly bound tightly together and knotted for all time.

"We can build on these foundations, Fritha. The Romans have given me a home again." He frowned and wondered, "Were they Christians? Or did they worship the old gods? We shall never know."

"The Archbishop himself will bless this place for us, Wolf, for it will remind him too of home." Then she shook her head. "If he is well enough. If he is ever well enough."

"Of course he will be well!" Wolf spoke roughly because he did not dare contemplate what was already being spoken, that the Archbishop would never live to see the completion of the monastery and the new church.

Fritha said, "His voice is too quiet, Wolf."

And this was the severest evidence she could offer of his declining strength, for his great harsh voice had been the trumpet call by which they had all fought and struggled and triumphed. . . .

Fritha's hands were covered with earth and torn

grass. The whiteness they had acquired in the Queen's service was quite hidden, and she held them out and cried in dismay.

But Wolf said, "That is how I like them. Strong and honest."

Fritha laughed. She scrambled to her feet.

"But they must be clean tomorrow. I am going back now, Wolf, or I shall be missed."

Before he could protest or so much as touch her hand, she had started to run away over the grass that was already theirs, back to the city and the Queen's dwelling, from which next day he would go to fetch her. She paused at last and turned back to wave and call to him:

"Tomorrow!"

"Tomorrow! Let it come soon!"

Alone, he pulled the mat of grass back over the paving. It was his and he wanted no prying eyes to covet it. He went slowly back and sought out Brother Adrian in the priory kitchens, where there was some tallying and calculating to be done before next week's market.

With Brother Adrian were Brother Lucius and one of the young English monks, Brother Britwald.

"The Archbishop was taken ill just after noon," Brother Adrian told Wolf.

"Seriously ill?"

"He does not speak, they say. He is hard pressed to breath."

Brother Lucius gave Wolf a rather wry smile. "Now,

the saints help us, who will make Wolf and Fritha man and wife?"

"I fear the ceremony cannot take place," said Brother Britwald.

"Ah well," said Brother Adrian, "maybe Wolf will change his mind now and become one of us after all."

Wolf flushed. He knew they were teasing him as they so often did. He was odd man out among all these religious and they never let him forget it. Even now, with the bad news of the Archbishop's health, they could not resist the joke.

"I will give you my fourth son," Wolf said. Then he laughed as their faces lit up. "No, it is *not* a solemn vow, Brothers! Who knows, I may have none but daughters—a poor lookout for a man with two fields, three cows, and a sow and a dozen geese!"

As they laughed quietly together, gently and easily as they had laughed often in the past, there was the sound of running feet, sandals slapping on stone, a man panting and muttering as he hurried by.

For a second the four of them there in the kitchen stood frozen, their faces turned toward the door, their voices stilled by the dreadful urgency of that hurrying.

Then before they could recover and cry out in dismay, they heard the great thunder of the bronze bell in the north tower. Once it boomed, and again. Then again, again, again. Slow, ponderous, spelling out a message too heavy to be quickly given.

Then under and below the big bell's clamor came

the quick ringing of the little summoning bell in the cloister. From all over the building the monks came hurrying, wringing their hands, weeping. There was no doubt how the summons must be interpreted.

Outside in the streets, in the city, in the country-side, men paused at the sound of the bell. They began to move at once toward the great gates of the priory. Women and children ran from the houses and joined the men, and the crowd increased moment by moment, surging toward the gates.

They knew the truth. They heard it in the bell's great mournful thunder. They came not to hope but to mourn. They had lost the man who had changed their lives and all their future and the future of their land; who had torn down their idols, rebuilt the ruined churches and temples and consecrated them afresh, in the name of God the Father, God the Son, God the Holy Ghost; who had brought consolation and content to the people and guided them in many practical ways.

As suddenly as he had come, he was gone. One day, it seemed, he had stepped onto their shore, a stranger whose words they could not understand; the next he was gone and they must do without him. Their hearts told them what their heads might have rejected, that they could not hope to see his like again. A stern man, who had never offered any one of them, less still himself, an easy way.

"God rest his saintly soul," said Brother Adrian. "Come to the chapel, Brothers. There will be much to do."

The three monks moved away silently, one after the other, leaving Wolf standing alone. An intense isolation touched him then. For all his friendship with them, his living close to the community all these years, at a moment of crisis he was nothing. They turned inward toward one another, in a sympathy he could not know, with a closeness he would never understand. For a second he longed to cry after them, to call that he would be one of them after all, that he might share the intensity of their experience and the depth of their prayers.

He heard his father's voice. "Wolf!"

"I am here."

"He is dead," said Wolfstan.

"I know it."

"Ah, you are young, you have your life, you have Fritha. But I have lost much in losing him. It was to come with him to England that I was given my freedom. How poorly I have paid my debt!"

"No, Father, no. You have done nobly. None could do more. But what will happen now?"

"God knows," said Wolfstan sadly and gently. "God knows. The whole world must miss him. He leaves us at a time of trouble. But the future will be built on his work."

Wolf smiled a little. He seemed to see the foundations Augustine had laid, and they were a little like the good solid pavement on which he and Fritha would build their enduring home.

Author Profile

BARBARA WILLARD (1909-1994) was born in Sussex, England. She enjoyed over fifty years of writing for both children and adults. Her father was an actor, and she made her first stage appearance at the age of eleven. After completion of her formal schooling, she continued acting, and in addition, began writing film scripts and novels for adults. In the late 1950's Miss Willard turned to writing for children, fulfilling a life-long desire. Her favorite genre was historical fiction, of which *Augustine Came to Kent* is an early example. Since she had been an only child until the age of twelve, many of her nearly sixty works reflect a fascination with large families. Of her later work, her personal favorites were the acclaimed Mantlemass series, which follow an English country family from the 1400's through 1600's.

Augustine Came to Kent was originally published by Doubleday in its Clarion Books series—a special set of titles written to present significant historical times and events from a Christian perspective. Miss Willard also wrote *Son of Charlemagne* and *If All the Swords in England* for this series.